Sofía's
Saints

Bilingual Press/Editorial Bilingüe

General Editor
 Gary D. Keller

Managing Editor
 Karen S. Van Hooft

Associate Editors
 Barbara H. Firoozye
 Thea S. Kuticka

Assistant Editor
 Linda St. George Thurston

Editorial Consultant
 Shawn L. England

Editorial Board
 Juan Goytisolo
 Francisco Jiménez
 Mario Vargas Llosa

Address:
 Bilingual Press
 Hispanic Research Center
 Arizona State University
 P.O. Box 872702
 Tempe, Arizona 85287-2702
 (480) 965-3867

Sofía's Saints

DIANA LÓPEZ

Bilingual Press/Editorial Bilingüe
TEMPE, ARIZONA

Library of Congress Cataloging-in-Publication Data

López, Diana.
    Sofia's Saints / Diana López.
        p. cm.
    ISBN 1-931010-07-2 (alk. paper)
    1. Mexican American women—Fiction. 2. Christian saints in art—Fiction. 3. Home ownership—Fiction. 4. Women artists—Fiction. 5. Single women—Fiction. 6. Waitresses—Fiction. I. Title.

PS3612.O62 S64 2002
813'.6—dc21

                                                                            2002071743

PRINTED IN THE UNITED STATES OF AMERICA

Cover and interior design: Aerocraft Charter Art Service

To Tricia

Why does this age seek a sign?
I assure you,
no such sign will be given it!

MARK 8:12

Acknowledgments

I would like to thank the faculty and students at the Southwest Texas Writing Program, especially Dagoberto Gilb and Tom Grimes whose advice and encouragement have proven immeasureable.

Much gratitude to everyone from Horace Mann and to Cristal Casarez and Cindy Sullivan.

Finally, but with the deepest affection, thanks to my family— Mom, Dad, Albert, Tricia, Steven—and to my husband, Gene, who so generously imbues my world . . . with magic.

The Market

I draw with fire. After all, isn't it in fire and through fire, the fire of that strange bush that will not be consumed, that God speaks His one absolute truth? I AM WHO I AM. My fire is not so mystical, is no more than the hot iron tip of a pyroelectric pen. I draw my own interpretations of saints—St. Anne, St. Dominic, St. Jude. Instead of in the blazes of hell, St. Lucifer stands in the oil refinery flames that stink up the edges of Corpus Christi. Instead of a child on his back, St. Christopher carries the Harbor Bridge and the Intercoastal Highway. Here in the musty building of the Trade Center Flea Market my woodburnings hang on the walls of my best friend's booth—For Sale.

"Sofía, you need to diversify," Susie says, her wispy mouth fattened by thick red lipstick. She's pretty in a girlish way, a prettiness that would be nice without the sexy attempt at makeup, without the bangs splayed upright like a fan. "You need logos. Pizza Hut or Budweiser. Spanish surnames written in calligraphy."

"Logos?" I say.

"Or a gimmick. Second one at half price or free gift wrapping like those people over there." She points to bins of Tupperware and Slim Jims across the aisle, her fingernail sculptured and drippingly red.

Susie is always thinking about maximizing profits. This whole flea market booth is her idea. She rents the space. She posts a sign above the doorway: Church Things. She sells baptism gowns, first communion veils, unity candles. She runs the kitchen sink to fill plastic vials while making the sign of the cross over her own version of holy water, and she can guiltlessly play the priest because no one cares about authenticity at the Trade Center Flea Market. People here believe in signs. Not the prophetic signs of God, but advertisements. The booth across the aisle sells generic purses, but for an extra ten the salesman adds a Dooney & Bourke tag. Looks like the real thing, the customers say, so pleased. No one can tell the real from the fake, so Susie doesn't flinch when old women buy her "holy" water to dab on their wrists like perfume. She dumps their change in the cash box while I glance at my woodburnings that wait for curious thumbs.

"What do you think?" Susie says. "I'm just trying to get you more money."

"I only draw saints. It's what I see in the wood."

"All I see are splinters and little gnarly things," she says, disgusted by my lack of ambition.

She complains about the heat, pulls at her blouse to let some air in. We have lived in Texas all our lives and should know the weather by now. Corpus Christi's heat thickens the air with humidity that clings to our hair and collects in the creases of our necks. We have air-conditioners and fans in the flea market, but their rotating and venting only stir the dampness. Already midday and I smell the sweat, the crowd's slight oniony odor mixed with cheap perfume and the dried-up pee from a dog chained to a nearby table leg. It stinks. That strange syrup of people clinging to each other. Young girls with their thumbs wrapped around their boyfriends' belt loops, mothers tugging at their children's raw wrists. Susie and I pick up xeroxed coupons for back rubs, facials, thirty-minute doses of UV radiation from the tanning salon. We fold them accordion style. We fan ourselves.

"I'll never look good in this heat," she says.

"Who cares?"

"I do. I've got a date with Frank after this."

"You mean Mr. Silver Tooth himself?" I tease.

"I told you. He got it in the army. That's how they fixed teeth back then."

"Back then? How old is he?"

"None of your business. At least I'm not robbing the cradle," she says, meaning my boyfriend, Julián, lanky Julián, only sixteen years old and me already thirty. He's not really my boyfriend, though. Just someone who comes by when he's bored. I bake for him. I let him watch TV. I give him twenty dollars when he changes my Suburban's oil, mows the lawn, smiles in a certain way that I like.

I know he's from the neighborhood somewhere. Sweeping a web from my porch, I saw him riding his bike and at the same time heard a snack truck blaring "Pop Goes the Weasel." I waved him over and gave him three bucks for some ice cream. He could have disappeared forever, but he came back five minutes later with two Eskimo Pies which we ate on the porch, vanilla drops on our shoes and chocolate shards sliding down our arms. I watched him lick one off his elbow's inner crook.

The first thing he said to me was, "You some kind of teacher?" and I laughed because I'd spoken so imperatively before.

He reminded me of Donatello's *David*—baked skin, long hair, his posture halfway girlish, his voice and physique caught between boy and manhood. He was all potential, like an unburned slab of wood.

"There's more to a man than his teeth," Susie says.

"Like what?"

"Romance," she sighs, wistfully resting her chin on that manicured hand of hers. I can't argue with that because Frank is an old-fashioned romantic. He buys her roses and boxed chocolates. He writes sentimental poems, memorizes Shakespeare sonnets at the bookstore while Susie sifts through *Glamour* magazines. *Let me not to the marriage of true minds,* he once wrote on a napkin. Susie doesn't know Shakespeare from a jingle on TV.

"You're his midlife crisis," I say, feeling mean. "Love is Dutch these days. You pay your way, I'll pay mine. No one owes a thing. Intimacy is sex on the couch with the TV on, a big-screen TV and Surround Sound stereo."

"You can't be serious," she says. "You think life is one big game."

"I know you, Susie. You have ulterior motives."

"Here we go," she says with an edge of exasperation. I stop talking because she's getting pissed off, and if that happens, she won't call, won't answer, won't let me apologize till she's sure I've suffered. I've known her since childhood. We did adolescent things together like curling our fingers into imaginary lips to practice our kissing, like folding our letters into footballs, stars, or fancy origami swans. She's the closest thing I have to family. She's taken care of me before and I love her for it. So why do I roll my eyes when she mentions Frank? It would be simple if we were teenagers again. She could act out her Cinderella scene and I'd believe it. But she's got ambitions, a fantasy that involves fancy cars, dinners at the Hershey Hotel, shopping sprees with a Gold Mastercard. Frank, the rich tycoon; Susie, the slut-in-waiting. He's only a nurse, but Susie pretends he's a doctor.

We hear a high-pitched voice screeching at us from the aisle. "¿Dónde están las flacas?" Chimuelita, my boss's wife, lumps toward us with plastic containers of food. I spend Saturdays at the flea market, ten to six, but during the week, I work at Pete's, a Mexican restaurant but really a bar. Pete is a real person, not just the name on the sign. He's the burly man who owns the place and Chimuelita is the cook.

"Such skinny girls," she says. "You have to give your señor something to squeeze." She sticks out her chest, but her breasts lost their perkiness years ago. "Look at this." She lifts the sombrero lid of a basket filled with warm tortillas. I tear off the edge of one, give her the rest. She rolls it between her palms and bites it with her molars.

"Who started calling you 'Chimuelita'?" Susie asks.

"Pete."

"Why?"

"Because my teeth fell out."

"But why did they fall out?"

"Ay, m'ija," she says. "It's the price I must pay for my promesas. Because each time I ask God or La Virgen for something, I give a tooth in return."

"You knock out your own teeth?" I ask.

"No, they just fall out when it's time. I keep them in a big mayonnaise jar." Susie and I glance at Pete, who's by the martial arts booth considering balisong knives and Benny "The Jet" karate books. "You don't think he knocked them out?" Chimuelita says, laughing, her breasts flopping like beached fish. "He might raise his voice, m'ijas, but he never raises his fists."

"You're crazy," we say, laughing too. This is what I like best about Chimuelita. She can take a little doubt and chase it away with a good laugh or a prayer. She slaps my shoulder affectionately, but it stings. She's like the ape that forgets its own strength when it plays.

"I want you to empty those bowls by the time I come back," she says, putting them behind the counter. She walks toward Pete and the people move aside in a way that looks deferential against her enormous size.

"Mind the fort," Susie says, "and I'll get us some Cokes from the snack bar."

She walks toward the scent of popcorn, peanuts, and Cornish hens on skewers, weaving her way through the crowd, her cropped blouse revealing the tanned sliver of her back as she parts mothers from their children and husbands from their wives. In her high-heeled shoes she looks like a girl playing dress-up.

In the afternoon the flea market is a sluggish place. A few customers walk in but only because ours is the least crowded booth. We've sold a few bookmarks and cards. It isn't the season for anything else. The thirtieth of September already. A dry time for sacraments. The catechism kids are just starting school and the wedding peak ended in July.

I smell hairspray and a minty stick of gum. A woman looks at the cards, reads a few, fans herself with the pastel envelopes. I ask if she needs help, but she ignores me. She drifts to my wall, contemplates the saints, picks out the guardian angel hovering above two children on a bridge, discarded drug needles and a television set in the ditch below.

"Shouldn't they be walking over water?" she says accusingly.

"Over danger."

"Well, you can't expect me to buy this thing, to hang it on my wall with little kids around." She gives me a hard look.

"The water was just a metaphor," I explain.

"But art should be pretty, don't you think? Decorative. Not ugly like this." She talks on, but her voice becomes merely noise amidst a whole market of noise—the intercom, the cashiers, the radio commercials, the man calling out from his booth, "Rolex Watches, fifty dollars, no checks please."

This is why I don't like paper—because it's thin, because it isn't like heavy, irregular scraps of wood that refuse to be framed, like me. The minty lady says I have no respect for art's necessary prettiness and with this stubborn assertion, fails to consider—just consider—something beyond the worn images on her TV and kitchen wall. She becomes paper-thin, and I can see through her makeup, clear through her head to the people in the aisle beyond. She leaves when she sees I'm not listening, turns her head sharply, her hair maintaining its stiff inanimacy. *I don't need your stupid money,* I think with conviction, and why *would* I need it except for rent and groceries?

"Catch," Susie says, tossing me a canned soda.

We open the Tupperware lids, inhale the aroma of carne guisada with rice and beans. We eat everything.

"A fat woman is a happy woman," Chimuelita says when she returns. She believes that a pregnant woman who walks in the full moon's light will bear a child with a big ugly mancha on its face. She believes that crossed legs in church are like crossed fingers during a promise, nullifying all the prayers and petitions. She believes that running out of salt in the kitchen causes bad luck for many years, more years than from breaking a mirror or walking beneath ladders. I used to be like her. I used to make the sign of the cross when passing Catholic churches, though I'm not sure why, since my mother never took me to church and insisted that God had a grudge against her.

"He could make the blind see and the crippled walk, but He couldn't give me the one thing I wanted."

"What was that?" I asked, thinking she wanted to spin straw to gold like the princess in the Rumpelstilskin fairy tale. She gave me the you-should-know look, which meant my father, that unnamed ghost between us. After waiting a few years for his return, she stopped going to church and started dating voraciously, fucking her boyfriends in the room next to mine, her door ajar, the radio too soft to drown out the tapping of the rosaries she hung from her bedposts. She took the mystery of sex and made it as mundane as mouthwash or deodorant. That's why I won't give myself to a man. The thought of it conjures up that image of my mother acting like some inanimate toy. She didn't even pretend to like sex. Some of those boyfriends might have married her, but she'd discard them before it ever reached that point.

"They aren't like him," she'd say.

Chimuelita fingers things in the booth, picks up vanilla-scented candles with the images of the Virgin Mary, Niño Fidencio, and the Sacred Heart of Jesus. She gets a glow-in-the-dark rosary, a few tiny pewter arms and legs for the altar, and a woodburning of St. Francis standing half-immersed in the ocean with his hand on the dorsal fin of a shark and a strange crustacean dangling from the rope that secures his frock.

"What's this?" Pete asks when he sees the items she's placed on the counter. He's a big man, a Mexican who somehow inherited that strange combination of dark skin and rusty hair growing along the rim of his balding head and in long, wiry sideburns.

"I'm going to buy them."

"And this?" He picks up my woodburning. "What kind of saint is this?"

"St. Francis."

"St. Francis? Where are the deer and birds?"

Chimuelita slaps his hands away. "There aren't any deer or birds. This is a work of art. Can't you see?"

Pete clenches his caterpillar brows and bites his lower lip as he turns the picture upside down, sideways, then upright again. The last thing he'll admit is not seeing what seems so obvious to his wife. "Aha," he says a little uncertainly. "We'll hang it upstairs."

The whole market empties out when Pete and Chimuelita leave and there's nothing to do but wait for six o'clock. I browse through the light green pages of Susie's ledger, its black intersecting lines, its rows of transactions printed in her perfect manuscript. She has a love for money, counting it two or three times a day, riffling through a dollar bill bundle and smelling it. We go to the sale racks at the mall and Susie calculates the prices of things, never trusts technology the way I do. Ten, twenty, forty percent off, and she has the total faster than the cashier can scan the UPC code. She went to college for this, to Career Point Business School in San

Antonio. "She's still off at college," her mother would say when I needed to borrow shoes, cry over a favorite show's cancellation, or eat barbecue with an intact family on a lonely Sunday afternoon. Susie's two years in San Antonio were the pits. I'd call her long distance despite the steep bill.

When I get home from the flea market, I dump my money in a big Maxwell House Coffee can. I don't drink coffee but my mother drank whole potfuls to get started in the morning. When she died, I kept the last can for a piggy bank. I'd seen commercials about coffee cans on tables with china, silverware, linen, and newly lit candles whose wax had not yet dripped down the sides. I relished the father inhaling his coffee on a porch swing next to his beautiful wife and cherubic children laughing at blond Labrador pups. *Maxwell House, good to the last drop.* Even though it's slowly rusting away, my can reminds me of that fantasy house—the floor that never needs the mop and broom, the back yard without flies, the coffee that wakes me with all the tenderness of a doting mom. Anytime I need some extra cash, I pull out a handful from my can and it's always enough. My one remaining superstition: Never count the change because to put a number on it is to limit it somehow. I have a loaves-and-fishes philosophy that by some grace of God my money will multiply when I need it. Sometimes I look at the coins and almost see halos circling the heads of the presidents.

I look out my window at the yard which is neat but uninspired in the way its sidewalk goes straight from the street to the door and divides my lawn into two squares of mostly dead grass. I've got a small house. I eat on a shaky card table, sit on the fold-up chairs or the lumpy sofa, watch a TV too big for the flimsy entertainment shelves. The kitchen sink is chipped and tea-stained, stalagmites of books clutter the floor, and wood scraps lie haphazardly like fallen leaves. I know this isn't worthy of *Better Homes and Gardens,* but it's my space and I can lock its doors against the world or leave them open.

"Sofía," I hear before I can sift through my mail. Julián peers through the screen door and tries to open it, but the latch catches first. I smell soap and Johnson's Baby Shampoo when a breeze runs through. He's got water beads on his arms because he hasn't dried off completely.

"Got anything to eat?" he asks, going to my pantry before I can answer and grabbing a bag of potato chips.

I don't have real food in my house—no bread or milk, no eggs to boil, though I like how they feel, their shells like stones polished by a river's currents and their springy, baby-smooth underskins. I once read a book in which a man gave a woman an avocado. I would like to give Julián something like that, to have enough soil in my yard for a garden, so I can dig my fingers into a home-grown tangerine, its scent filling the room as I feed it to him, the segments bursting in his mouth like the centers of bonbons. He's too thin. When he sits with his elbows on the table, he's nothing but a hungry line feeding on potato chips and Coke.

I microwave a bag of popcorn and, instead of tangerine segments, I throw kernels at his open mouth. When one hits his cheek, he picks it up and throws it back at me, starting a food fight, our air-puffed pellets flying and making us laugh so we don't hear Mr. Vela at the door until he clears his throat in that please-excuse-me way. He's already removing his cowboy hat when I let him in and his hair stays dented from its rim. He wears what he always wears: Wranglers, a white guayabera, a chain with Jesus hanging from a gold anchor. If I know what a father should be, it's because of Mr. Vela, my landlord, who always rescues me, who fixes things—leaking pipes, broken windows, clogged drains—who gives me first bid on his garage sale stuff and all his cast-off machinery—a stereo, a washing machine, even my Suburban, that gas-guzzling rust bucket that somehow gets me from point A to B. When I was a child, he gave me a jewelry box with a plastic ballerina twirling on a spring, her toes like upright carrots. *Dance of the Sugar Plum Fairy* would chime and she would pirouette even after the paint had rubbed off her plastic tutu and the diamond-shaped mirror fell away. When something in her little box fell loose, Mr. Vela fixed it and put the spin back into her.

"Where are your tools?" I say because I left a message about the door's torn screen.

"I'm not here for that."

He steps in tentatively. Out of respect for me or because of some old-fashioned rule of courtesy, Mr. Vela still waits for my invitation before entering or sitting down.

"You her uncle or somethin'?" Julián says after a few seconds of curious staring.

"This is Mr. Vela," I say, "my landlord."

Julián eyes him suspiciously, and when he decides that Mr. Vela isn't a threat, he stuffs a handful of popcorn in his mouth and then eats the kernels that landed on the table and couch. "Well, I'll see you later," he says, walking out, mounting his bicycle and riding off.

"What's going on here?" Mr. Vela asks when Julián turns the corner.

He looks at the popcorn scattered on the floor with a curiosity that makes me feel defensive. "He's just a kid from the neighborhood. He comes by to mow the lawn sometimes. I made a bag of popcorn and he started throwing it around," I add to explain the mess. "You know how kids are these days."

I don't know what Mr. Vela is really thinking, but he lets it go, settles on the couch, his palms on his knees, his fingers tapping nervously, his posture too stiff and upright, like a lawyer bearing bad news. He finds a scrap of woodburning on the coffee table, picks it up, turns it over, and sweeps the dust off.

"You want some tea?" I ask.

He doesn't answer. Nostalgically, he says, "I was thinking about the moldings on the door. How I put them there years ago when my wife and I got married. I was thinking about my son busting his lip on the edge of the table and the little Chihuahua that lost its eye and my wife's first sewing machine. All the things that happened here and belonged here. Like that old tire swing in the backyard. Remember that?" It's okay, I'm thinking, this little chat of ours, but there's something in his voice that makes me want to confirm my own experiences here.

"I remember climbing on the roof to see the fireworks on New Year's Eve," I say, "and falling on a backyard nail, getting stitches and a tetanus shot. I remember all the times I washed clothes here. Did your wife hang out clothes on the line? Did she ever pluck off the chicharra shells when she lived here a long time ago?"

He puts the woodburning down, runs his fingers through his hair. Sometimes we talk over a cup of tea, but today he's not giving me eye contact. "You see," he says, "I'm going to sell the house."

"Sell the house?" For a moment I wonder if the scene with Julián has pushed him to this, if he thinks I'm too irresponsible to live here.

"My wife and I are getting old," he explains. "We want to buy a Winnebago."

"You want to sell the house for a Winnebago?" I don't see the purpose, don't see how a home can equal an RV, but then it hits me—that fine line between friendship and business. I remember my mother's frustration, her hints for central air, her anger for things Mr. Vela had no control over like breaks in the water main and the ceiling leak that ruined her armoire.

"We want to travel," he says. "To Disneyland and Las Vegas. To see what America's all about."

"America?" I say, getting sassy again. "You can see America on TV."

He sees my clenched jaw, sighs like a shame-faced boy, weighs things on that invisible scale of his—like his concept of me, Sofía the tenant against Sofía the friend—his right to this house against mine. Ultimately he pits me against the Winnebago, me against a lumbering box on wheels. I start to see through him, through that furrowed brow, through the thick bowl of his skull. He must be imagining the American highways—the Nevada desert, Mount Rushmore, Louisiana swamps—and camping out along some roadside park cooking sausages over a propane stove, sleeping in a bed that folds out from a wall, gassing up at Texaco while he wipes away the smeared bodies of moths from his windshield. It's not fair. I've lived here longer than his family. If Mr. Vela and I were to stack our years here side by side, there would be no argument. My footsteps have worn the carpet in the hallway. My hands have dropped the plates that chipped the kitchen's tiles. It's my own opening and closing of doors that has loosened them from their hinges. This house is mine. I'm the one who understands its quirks. I know that the hot and cold are reversed on the bathroom sink, that the toilet must be flushed gently or it will run, that certain floorboards creak.

11

"And you have to lift the door with your foot," I find myself saying. "It's the only way to lock the deadbolt. Did you know that, Mr. Vela? Did you know the door sags?"

"My wife and I have always planned this," he says firmly.

"Of course," I snap back. "It's the American dream."

Part of my rudeness is fear. I've never considered living anywhere else. Mr. Vela looks at me with his calm brown eyes, and I feel guilty for being curt, for acting like a toddler whose lollipop's been taken away. I thought he'd watch over me forever.

"I have to do repairs," he says, "but I'll give you a chance before I put it on the market."

"A chance for what?"

"To buy it. I'll give you a good deal. I'll fix the place up for you."

"How much are you asking for?" I ask.

"At least fifty thousand."

"That's all it's worth?" I say even though I know it's an insurmountable amount for my salary.

"It's a modest house," he says. He walks to the screen door, stops there for a minute. "I won't sell it," he repeats, "without first giving you a chance."

I once asked if Mr. Vela were my grandfather. "No," my mother said. "He's not your grandfather at all," and this "at all" part of her statement was to keep me from pretending in even the smallest way—because it was dangerous, I guess—because she had a hard time working and raising a child and sleeping alone at night—because it was probably belief in a fantasy that got my mother pregnant in the first place. Maybe that was what she aimed to keep me from—the disappointment—the deep-down pit of disillusionment. I've seen men before, gone through the motions of dating, but not without waiting for that final letdown—and there has always been a letdown—a walking away and a slamming door.

After pitying myself for a few hours, I turn the TV on because it's the best way to forget things. Flipping through channels, I hear those myriad voices—cartoons, newscasters, Disneyland's *Let us remember the magic*, the weekend fishing report, talk show gossip, reports of drive-bys in Molina. An athlete with Nike high-tops jumps over a skyscraper, a Persian cat nibbles delicately at a scoop of food in a crystal glass, two lovers roll in the sand, breathe in not the scent of fish and seaweed, but of perfume. I finally settle on a fairy-tale cartoon, Hansel and Gretel already in the candied house, the witch feeding the fire with wood. I can tell they feel safe by the way they lick their lollipops—the long swipes and closed eyes. I switch channels again, find a cable show featuring exhibits from London, Paris, and New York. White canvases painted with off-white strokes, urinals with mildew rings, vacuum-filter lint glued to cardboard and framed, a critic's voice commenting on how the art represents the sanctity of bodily refuse, the rights of skin flakes, shed hair, dirt from the streets, and food crumbs, how none of these deserves to be ignored. Then I see a cow cross-sectioned in six equal slices and preserved in vats of Windex blue formaldehyde. Each sliver of lung or heart or intestine costs $40,000.

"What a joke," I say to myself.

I go to my table, take out a sketch pad because sometimes I can get ideas by drawing the wood's grain on paper first. There has to be some invention, a cooperation between artist, medium, subject. For me the process is slow. I stare into the wood—the walnut or basswood—each piece with its own hue, its own grain, its own saint floating from the rings. Drawing with my pyroelectric pen is nothing more than tracing an image already in the wood, making the saints evident to Susie, to Julián, to the flea market shoppers who can't see the holiness in nature the way I try to see it. I stare into this wood before me, draw its grain, till I see a shrouded Lazarus emerging from the dark entrance of an abandoned store, big windowpanes on either side of him, toppled mannequins and sale signs, a briefcase in his hand, and "Sold" on a billboard above.

I hoped that drawing would help me shake the image of that cross-sectioned cow, but even at night in my room, the sheets crumpled at the foot of my bed, the digits glowing green on the clock, the whines of dogs as the ambulances pass, the thought of $40,000 for a slice of cow haunts me. I mumble the rosary, count off Hail Marys with my fingers, think of Mr. Vela and this house and a sliced cow called art, because $50,000 is a lot of money for a waitress who sells saints on the side.

CHAPTER 2

La Sandía Queen

S treet people loiter around the garbage bins at Pete's. Uncombed women with threads hanging from unraveling seams and unshaven men with smoke-and-stale-meat breath huddle beneath trash bags to keep the rain off. When the sun returns, they'll scour the ground for cigarette butts, beer cans, food.

Pete's place is near Emerald Beach where a hospital and a Holiday Inn overlook the bay. The windows are tinted and barred, and the paint on the plywood placard that bears Pete's name is peeling off, is no longer red but a weak rust. It's a two-story building with the restaurant on the first floor and Pete's family living on the second. Facing the parking lot is a mural of La Virgen de Guadalupe, her image no different from what I've seen in all the books—a blue cape with stars, brilliant sun spokes radiating behind her, a child peeking from beneath her red robe's hem, and plump Mexican cherubs floating in the sky. There are sheets of rain on my windshield and she seems to tremble on the other side. I imagine her nose running and her fingers and toes puckered. I once wanted to erase the mural's black lines and make La Virgen's cape merge with the sky. "But what do you know about art?" Pete said. "You're a waitress."

I rush out of my car, the hard rain stinging. Pete's restaurant is cold, the ceiling fans almost rattling themselves loose and the thermostat uncomfortably low. Pete sweats anyway. He always has pale yellow splotches on his shirts' underarms, and he often dabs his forehead with a towel.

I've known Pete and Chimuelita for twelve years, got the job after Susie saw me pour a glass of clumping milk.

"You'll starve," she said, "if you don't start working."

I ate and slept at her house for three months after my mother died, but I needed to return home because Susie was leaving for San Antonio. She told me to put on a dress, and then she drove me to Pete's restaurant because of its Help Wanted sign. I sat in the car for three chickenshit minutes before Susie urged me out. "You'll have to go by yourself," she said, impatient.

I went in and saw Pete picking his nose and then sheepishly accepting a Kleenex from his wife.

"You here to order?" he asked when he caught me staring.

"I'm here because of the Help Wanted sign."

He gave me an up-down look. "You got a résumé?"

"A what?"

"A résumé—typed real neat saying what you can do."

"No, sir. My friend just drove me over."

He scratched his bald spot, gave me another up-down look, and told me to follow him to his office, which was actually a large janitorial closet with two chairs, a black-and-white TV, a Playboy calendar stuck in the previous December, and a desk with dead ivy in a toilet-shaped planter and several yellowing seek-and-find magazines. He rummaged through a drawer for something to write with, finally settling on a purple crayon and a used manila folder.

"What's your name?" he asked.

"Sofía Loren Sauceda," I said, embarrassed by the allusion to the actress. What was my mother thinking? Why couldn't she name me after a relative or a saint like most mothers do?

"How old are you?"

"Eighteen."

"Eighteen? You're not even old enough to serve beer." He rubbed his forehead as if I'd given him a migraine. "You at least have some experience?"

"No."

He put the purple crayon down. "Have you ever looked for a job before?"

"No," I said.

"Because in a real business establishment like this, you got to call first, make an appointment. It could save us both some time. That's what phones are for—and calendars," he said, pointing to the buxom Santa Claus. "You understand?"

"Yes, sir," I said, realizing he wasn't going to give me the job. I stared at the way his robust breathing rippled the red bristles beneath his nose, heard his half-scolding voice, and felt alone in the world—no mother and no marketable skill. I started blubbering, and Pete bolted out the door screaming for Chimuelita till we heard her flapping chanclas and high-pitched "¿Qué pasó?"

Pete panicked. "She just started crying," he blurted.

Chimuelita rolled up one of the seek-and-finds and swatted his back like he was some mischievous dog. "What did you do, cabrón?"

"Nothing," he said, shrugging. "It's like she's got some sort of cry switch." He grabbed a roll of toilet paper from a mountain of Charmin in the corner so I could blow my nose.

"Why are you crying?" Chimuelita asked in a gentle voice.

"It's just that my mother died in a car accident," I said, "and I don't have a father, either."

"No mother? No father?" She knelt before me.

"And my friend said I'd starve if I didn't get a job because she's leaving for San Antonio and I'll have no one to stay with." I dropped my head onto her sagging breasts and she stroked my hair like I was a puppy.

"Well, you're in luck," she said. "There's no reason why you can't work here."

"Here?" Pete protested. "She can't work the bar! She can't wait tables!"

"Can she ask people what they want?" Chimuelita said, standing and getting in his face. "Because that's all it is, Pete. Asking people what they want and bringing it in a timely manner." She waited till he nodded his consent.

"So I can have the job?" I said, hopeful.

"And dinner too," Chimuelita replied. "Pete will fill out your paperwork right away."

She flip-flopped out the door. Pete watched till her swaying hips turned a corner. "That's a whole lot of woman," he said before writing my address, telephone, and social security number with his purple crayon. I've been working and eating dinner with them ever since.

Except for Susie and Frank at a corner table, the restaurant's dead. Pete flips through the channels of a TV mounted above the bar—ABC, NBC, PBS, and Univisión, where he stops. The tracking is off. The actors float up and reappear at the bottom of the screen. He slaps the sides. "This thing screws up every time it rains!"

His son César gives a muffled laugh as he polishes a glass at the bar. He's only twenty-two, the youngest and shiest of four boys, and I suspect the least ambitious by the way Pete yells at him all the time. Pete sometimes seems like an overbearing father, but his boys have done well for themselves. One is a pharmacist, the other a school administrator, the third a computer technician. Pete paid their college tuition, but they had to do their time in the restaurant by busing tables and mixing drinks when they were old enough. "No free rides" is Pete's motto. The older sons learned how to juggle glasses and balance bottles on their heads to give the customers a show, but César isn't as entertaining. He grudgingly studies accounting—Pete's idea—but what César really wants to do is fish. He wants to wake up at four in the morning, watch the sun rise from a shrimp boat, and sort his catch at the T-heads, the piers where the fishing boats dock, while the tourists walk by and marvel at the slimy pink bodies in his hands. He doesn't mean to fish for a living, just wants to work at Pete's so he can have the leisure to fish. He's content without money as long as he has a roof, food, and time. I can understand that. But Pete's a different story, argues that César can do anything he wants as long as it's a step up from where he came from. It's an old argument. "He might hate accounting," Pete says, "but he'll hate it from a very nice house with a well-fed stomach, and he certainly won't stink like a dead fish." They've argued a million times, Pete yelling against César's timid protestations; meanwhile, César goes to school and drops glasses when he lets his mind wander. I wait for him to run off and join the fishing boats, but it won't happen. Pete's got a hold on his sons. If he asked them to sweep the floor with a hairbrush, they'd get down on their knees.

I grab a towel and dry off beneath the metal objects that hang from the restaurant's ceiling—umbrella frames, a machete, bicycle wheels, hubcaps, a few shallow washtubs. Pete has small square tables haphazardly arranged with single-stem carnations and votive candles in red bowls. He lets these candles burn out and, in the pool of the remaining wax, the blackened wicks stand upright like seared trees. He even lets the flowers dry out in their Corona bottle vases, the water green from their mildewing stems. In the back corner of the restaurant is a clearing topped by a neon-vested jukebox where people dance sometimes.

The only other evening employee is Parker. He's got long blond hair that he keeps in a braid, contacts to make his eyes look blue, and a few chicken pox scars on his face. He plays more than works, trying to learn Spanish and telling jokes that send Pete into a coughing fit of laughter. "What do you see when the Pillsbury doughboy bends over?" Parker says, "Doughnuts!" Pete laughs hard, slaps Parker's shoulder, writes down the joke for future reference. "You're OK," Pete says, and Parker might get a free drink after that or an extra plate of food.

I hear every word they say, but Parker's more private with César, who seems to disappear, to become a stool, a column, a chair. It's an unspoken tidbit that they've got something going on, and this surprises me because it's not like Pete the macho man to accept that his son's got a boyfriend. They disagree about everything else, but this topic never comes up. Pete even treats Parker like family already.

"Hey," Pete says to me, "what's up with your friend?" He points to Susie snuggling with her silver-toothed man. She likes her blouses low even though she's too flat chested for cleavage. She and Frank look at each other lovingly, I suppose. He takes a strand of her hair, twirls it around his finger, and when he lets go, it's in a knot. They laugh. It's so funny, this knot of theirs.

I can see how easy it is for Susie to fall into a fantasy about him. He's an RN in a clinic, but according to Susie, his job is just

19

a stepping-stone. She fancies him a doctor, a cardiologist doing pacemaker installations, triple bypasses, cardiac transplants. She pushes him on this, saying over and over how much she'd like him to go to medical school, how he has the brains for it. She doesn't get it—there's no romance in medicine. Doctors think the heart is simple, no more than tubes and valves, a mere pump, certainly not something to write poems for. She should leave him alone. He seems happy at the clinic, a state-funded place with lots of flirty viejitas.

"Look who's here," Susie says when she sees me. I sit beside her. There's no one to wait on, anyway. "I got an idea," she says before I can tell her about my house. She holds her hands up like a director framing a scene. "Picture this. A patient dressed as the Tin Man goes to Frank for a new heart. Get it?"

"Frank's the wizard?"

"The cardio-wizard. That's what we're going to call the practice," she says, never mind that he's only a nurse right now. "I had a brainstorm, Sofía, a virtual brainstorm." I have to do this—wait for a break in her speech before I can get my own thoughts out. Even when I'm desperate, when I say Susie we need to talk, I must first endure her silly conversations. She rattles on about a commercial for a store she doesn't have, Susie standing like Moses before a parted Gulf of Mexico, a slogan in an Old English font, Church Things, Where Miracles Are Cheap! "What do you think?" she asks, turning toward Frank for his opinion.

"I think you're going to need a permit to part the Gulf," he says, and she laughs hard, tells him that he has such a sense of humor.

Frank is still in his clinic clothes, pale blue scrubs and a stethoscope around his neck. She takes it, pulls his neck forward for a kiss, refuses to let him go. He sits like a pet on a leash, gently plucks away her fingers, holds them in his lap. When she needs her hand for some lipstick, he keeps it, tells her she has to pay the toll, a kiss with a nuzzling of noses.

"Mr. Vela's going to sell the house," I say, interrupting their intimate moment. Susie pulls away from him and swipes her lips with a clownish red.

"Just like that?" she says nonchalantly.

"He says I can buy it from him."

"For how much?"

"Fifty thousand."

"Fifty thousand? That's all?" She puts two fingers in a votive bowl and crushes the candle's charred wick. "It's no big deal, Sofía. You just go to the bank and apply for a mortgage loan." No big deal? Life is so easy according to her. She keeps her mind on light things, and I remember that her name is Susie after all, that it has no formal version of itself, no Susan or Susana or Suzanne lurking behind the diminutive.

She's too much like my mother sometimes. I remember coming home once to an eighteen-wheeler cab parked in front of my house. It didn't have its trailer and its flat end looked like the rump of a dog without a tail. Neighborhood kids were marveling at the huge tires and running their hands across the radiator grille. Little girls were trying to sit like the white silhouettes of the Playboy bunnies on the mud flaps.

When I went inside, I saw my mother full of makeup and hair-spray. She teetered in her heels. She had that let's-play-dress-up quality about her even though she was a grown woman already. "Look who's here," she said, nodding to a man at the table.

"Is this *her*?" he asked. My mother had lots of boyfriends, but the way this man said "her," with a punch, made me think he was my father, someone my mother never explained except to say that he'd come around someday.

"Where do you live?" was all I could say.

"In the truck."

"In the truck? You mean you don't have an address?" I asked because I needed to pin him down, make him less elusive.

"I have a post office box," he said, "in Cotula."

He took out a present I was too old for, a doll wrapped with comic strips and masking tape. So this was my father sitting at the table in Levi's and a flannel shirt, with grease beneath his nails, with heavy working boots, without a stay-put address. He was oily and flabby from sitting in the truck too much.

"You got a lot of friends at school?" he asked.

"Sure," I said, not wanting to tell him that my classmates called me "Grace" because my limbs were stretching faster than my torso, because of the graceless way I walked and did my jumping jacks.

"She likes to draw," my mother said in a chimelike voice. She placed trays of deviled eggs, nachos, rolled slices of ham and turkey, diced cheese, and potato chips before him. She never liked cooking hearty meals. She preferred snacks and appetizers, which is all I ever learned to make. The man hovered above his food, chomping noisily, licking fingers that stayed shiny after being in his mouth.

I said accusingly, "Are you my father?"

"Is that what you've been telling her?" he asked my mother, laughing as if it were such a charming thing for a woman to do.

"No," she answered, throwing me a scolding glance. "She just likes to pretend." She waited on him like some weightless fairy, put three more nachos on his plate, and I wondered *who was really pretending?* She could take any man, make him a prince, and forget that his keys were jingling in his impatient hands, yet she'd never let me believe in once-upon-a-times.

Susie's no different. She allows herself big dreams about Frank, but when I tell her about my house, all she gives me is down-to-earth talk about mortgage loans and interest rates. All I can think of is a number, Mr. Vela's concrete, non-negotiable amount, a five and four impossible zeros. Susie's got her boyfriend's arm around her shoulder and two parents still alive, and all I have is a rusting Suburban and an apron hanging from a nail on Pete's wall.

"You know," Frank says, "I can buy some of your wood things."

"My wood things?" I repeat, pissed because he doesn't call them art.

"Sure. You can make that medical sign with the snakes for all my friends. I can give them away as Christmas gifts."

"He's got a lot of doctor friends," Susie says.

"Make me ten and I'll pay you fifteen dollars apiece."

"You're such an angel," Susie says, grabbing his stethoscope and pulling his neck forward again. "You're a bona fide saint."

I can only roll my eyes as they play their patty-cake games. She thinks this is going to last forever? I saw my mother with her boyfriends. I know what men are all about. There was magic for two months or two weeks. Then they got on top of her, moving around while she lay beneath them struggling to find their rhythm with her hips. There can't be mystery in a man once he's taken off his clothes, once he's sat at the bed's edge, run his fingers through his hair, shaken out the wrinkles from his discarded shirt. Frank's not a saint, not even a doctor. He's got a limited cash flow like everybody else. Beneath that silver tooth is nothing but a cavity slowly rotting away.

"So you'll do it?" Susie asks.

"No, but if he wants, I can sell him my picture of St. Barbara."

"St. Barbara? You can't hang that thing in a doctor's office!" She laughs like it's a joke, though I meant to be sarcastic. In my picture, St. Barbara lies on an operating table, her eyes rolled back and her tongue lolling from the anesthesia. Instead of getting her head lopped off by a sword, she gets it removed by a doctor with a scalpel. The doctor's hair, hands, mouth, and nose hide behind sterilized cloth, and his only proof of humanity is the greedy expression behind his plastic medical goggles.

"I'll buy ten St. Barbaras," Frank says.

"Ten?" I repeat. "I couldn't make ten for a hundred or even a million dollars. My saints are wood-specific. I can't force an image where it doesn't belong."

The little bell of Pete's door jingles, and a man in jeans and a Travis School polo shirt walks in, wipes his feet on the welcome mat, and shivers briefly in the air-conditioned cold. The rain slows to a drizzle, and the sun begins to appear, the wet surfaces outside the windows giving everything a Monet-like indistinctness. The light behind the man makes a mysterious shadow of his face, and when he shakes his hands, the rainwater falls from them like magic dust from a wizard's fingertips.

"Who's that?" Susie says, pinching my arm when she sees me staring.

"Someone to wait on," I say, grudgingly standing up.

Pete calls out, "Are you the guy from the classifieds?"

"Yes," the man says, moving into the bar's light, and I recognize him. It's David from my days at Del Mar College. He was an education major, but he also took art classes.

"That's the difference between you and me," I told him once. "You draw the way an old man solves a crossword puzzle—on weekends, without bothering to fill in all the spaces, making up words when you don't know the answers."

"In other words, I'm half-assed," he said.

"Half-ass is right."

He told me I was too holier-than-thou about art and he was probably right. I took every art and English class the college had to offer, and when I was through, I dropped out. Why waste time on the core curriculum? I went to study what I loved—pictures and stories—to catch a glimpse of what made people believe in gods and magic spells.

But David and I were good friends. We'd sit on the library steps to argue about books, we'd play ping-pong at the Harvin Student Center, watch intramural basketball games, or share snow cones on unbearably hot days. Sometimes we sat on the floor of the music building's hallway and listened to the dissonance of instruments tuning up, the choir's catlike vocal drills, the trials and errors of new musicians. Sometimes I'd hear a faint melody beneath the noise, and I knew, I positively knew, that David listened to the same muted melody, and when we'd leave, we'd cling to that shared intimacy by meandering the grounds in silence.

Then he screwed things up by asking me on a real date, something I'd have to dress up for, play the giggly fairy for like my mother did. I said, "Can't we be just friends?" the lamest, most cliché line I could give a man. He was polite and patient, but I didn't know what to say after that, didn't want him to think there was something under the friendship, something that would lead to sex, so I started giving sarcastic answers to everything he asked. It worked, I guess. He stopped meeting me at the library steps, stopped playing ping-pong, disappeared when the days were unbearably hot. I missed the way he knew the names of plants, the way he squinted when he blushed. Damn him. Because sitting in the music hallway alone, there was no melody, nothing but noise and the echoes of noise, nothing but my ass getting numb from the cold, hard floor.

"Ándale, Sofía," Pete calls and David turns around, mildly surprised. We throw weak smiles at each other, but what can we say after eight or nine years? For the moment we pretend to be strangers.

Pete asks me to get some drinks from his "special stock," an icebox in the kitchen where he keeps imported beer. When I return, Chimuelita is arguing with him, saying, "What about Sofía?"

"What about me?" I ask.

"Sofía can't paint," Pete says. "She's a waitress."

"And what do you call her St. Francis, cabrón?"

"Drawing little wood things is not the same as painting walls."

"What wall?" I ask.

"The wall outside the restaurant," Pete says. "I want Selena there. This man's going to paint it."

I can't believe Pete wants to wash out La Virgen and paint a two-story Selena, Corpus Christi's Tejano music queen, whose face is everywhere already—on T-shirts, billboards, notebooks that girls carry to school. *Selena,* for rent at the video store. *Hurry, while supplies last.*

Susie hears the commotion, comes over, starts arguing my case too. "That's not fair," she says. "Sofía went to college for art."

"We could work together," David offers.

"No," I say. "The last thing I want to do is paint Selena. I only draw saints."

"But Selena *is* a saint," Chimuelita says. Pete shakes his head, extends a hand to David, who takes it and promises to begin right away after I ignore another imploring look.

"It's not right," Susie argues as if Pete's doing me some great injustice. "Sofía needs the money to buy her house."

"What are you talking about?" Pete says. "I own the place. This town's been torn up ever since Selena died. Don't blame me for wanting to honor her somehow. Hey, Parker." He tosses a quarter. "Put some Selena music on the jukebox. Give this man some inspiration." He gets behind the bar, pours his "special" beer in a frozen glass, and hands it to David. "Here's some more inspiration," he says.

I follow Chimuelita to the kitchen, grab my apron, and sit beside her at the counter where she rolls her globs of masa into tight little balls for the tortilla machine. I help her when business is slow. We're silent, Chimuelita too reverent to speak while Selena sings, and we fall into the quiet rhythm of our work.

What Chimuelita and Susie fail to understand, what I tried explaining before when Frank wanted to buy ten St. Barbaras, is that I can't paint something where it doesn't belong. Sometimes I stare from the inner side of Pete's wall and can feel the weight against it, the leaning drunkards, the tired women waiting for the bus, the young couples squirming in each other's arms. Sometimes I can sense the light pelts of debris against the bricks, green or brown shards, crushed cans, yard-sale signs from the telephone poles. On cold nights, the air seems to seep through the chipped masonry, and the only thing between me and the rough world outside is not a wall at all but the painted wisps of La Virgen's hair.

I remember the first time Julián saw my saints. He said, "I'm an artist too—me and my friends."

I thought it was a teenage boast until he introduced me to three boys standing cool in their knee-length shirts and Red Wing boots, a bad-ass way of leaning back, of losing their hands in their cargo pant pockets.

"Julián says you can give us a ride," one said.

"Downtown."

"To paint something." That's how they spoke, a series of voices for one line.

I was curious about the tomato crate with old spray paint cans—red, blue, yellow, three black—so I let them in my Suburban where they silently directed me with their pointing fingers. It was a hot Sunday afternoon, and downtown was a dusty, dark ghost town except for the custodians at a bank, a bridal boutique, and a few raunchy clubs. Only the Greyhound bus station was open for business.

"Pull in there," one said, pointing to an alley behind a long deserted Frost Brothers store.

They took their shirts off, tied them around their waists, then lined up their cans as neatly as bowling pins. They painted the Frost Brothers wall like they spoke, in series. One took the black can, vigorously shook it, and drew a squiggle which meant nothing until the other boys completed it. I sat across the alley, slapped at mosquitoes, caught an occasional whiff of meat rotting in a nearby dumpster, shooed away dogs who then chased wind-blown bags or sniffed discarded rubbers. I watched the sun's light reddening in the glistening sweat of the boys' backs and an intense moment of orange that made them seem afire. They worked without conferring and I found myself desperate to share their silent speech.

"What do you think?" they asked, showing me their version of Selena. They needed to point a flashlight by then so I saw their mural in a moving circle of light. I was impressed. They had painted Selena half-immersed in Padre Island's sand and hardly recognizable except for her long hair, disco clothes, and microphone. Seagulls stood about with pieces of her in their beaks—strands of hair, a shred of cloth, the strap of her high-heeled shoe. One pecked the microphone, and another scratched the sand where her nail peeped through.

"I like it," I said even though the painting was more cartoonish than real. "It makes perfect sense since seagulls are such scavengers."

They seemed confused, and I realized that they expressed themselves concretely, through clothes, posture, art. They didn't try pinning down meaning with words.

"Let's sign it," they said, taking the black paint and scribbling four spades at the bottom corner.

"You're gangbangers?" I accused.

"Taggers," they corrected.

"We just like to paint."

"It gets 'cleaned up' anyway."

"Cleaned up?" I asked.

"Some people from the neighborhood will probably paint over it in a couple of weeks."

"We don't really care if it doesn't last forever."

At first I wondered why they'd go to so much trouble, but then I understood that they cared only for the excitement of painting on the sly and for the experience of art rather than art itself. I felt a certain kinship to them. They gave me high-fives when we parted.

The music from the jukebox stops and the restaurant stays hushed except for Susie and Frank's laughter.

"Tell me how you and Pete met," I say to Chimuelita because I don't want to think about my house or David or Pete's wall. I've

27

heard the story a million times before, but Chimuelita has a way of telling a story that makes me forget the world.

"The farmers would get their biggest watermelon," she says, "and rub Vaseline all over it. They'd throw it into a pool, and the girl that got it from the water and carried it back got to be the Sandía Queen. So there I was, on a float in a green dress with a big sandía crown on my head."

"A sandía crown?"

"The ugliest thing you ever saw. Shaped like a piece of watermelon. Red sequins glued all over. And there were little sandía fairies throwing packets of watermelon seeds at the crowd. We had other queens too—the Cotton Queen and the Wheat Queen and the Bluebonnet Queen and even an Oil Queen."

"Tell me about the Oil Queen," I say.

"A poor girl too fat for a real float. Her father worked on the oil rigs. He paid the officials to let her ride in the back of his truck. She wore a black dress and sat on a rocking chair that almost tipped over every time they hit the potholes."

"And Pete?"

"Him? He was standing by the street with two buddies. They saw me waving at the crowd." She demonstrates, her hand white with flour. "Right away, they started fighting over me. I didn't know why at first. I knew them from school and all they ever did was make fun of my flour-sack dresses. But the costume made me pretty. They wanted to take me out, but my father said that no respectable girl would date three boys at a time." The image of Chimuelita with three boys fussing over her makes me laugh. "I had to choose," she says with complete seriousness. "And quick too because I knew they were in love with my watermelon dress, and the rules said you could only be the Sandía Queen once." She puts her hand on my shoulder. "Mira, m'ija, I prayed like I never prayed before. I asked God for a sign, and the next day when I looked out my window, there it was."

"A sign?" I ask.

"A chicken, Sofía. A real chicken in a tree." She takes a deep breath. "Chickens don't fly, and this one had grown up in my back yard without even looking at the sky." She does the sign of the cross. "It was a message from God. That chicken was red and

28

there was Pete with a head full of red hair. I plucked off a feather and gave it to him just to make sure the magic didn't wear off when he saw me in my flour-sack dresses again. Now we're married. Now I feel like the Sandía Queen all the time . . ."

She goes on, but I'm no longer listening. I think about it. I say it over and over in my mind, a message from God.

We hear the jukebox again, a Spanish tune, a combination of heavy bass, an accordion, and a singer whose Spanish carries a Texan lilt. The song's about paying quarters for kisses on the cheek from beautiful women called Beatríz, Marta, and Isabel. I return to the diner where Parker stands by the jukebox, claps his hands, taps his feet. He sings "bésame" like the song, but it sounds too much like "sesame" as in *Sesame Street*.

"It isn't about Big Bird," Pete says, coughing with laughter.

Pete and Parker share jokes at the jukebox, César fiddles with the mute TV, Susie and Frank flirt over a pitcher of beer, and though I'm not facing him, I worry that David's eyes are making their judgments and scoffing at my waitressing job, the same job I had when I knew him before, not that he's ever come by to visit. I worry about my appearance, my hair still long but not as sleek, my hips never having achieved their womanly curves, my fidgety hands. I venture a glance, but instead of looking at me, he's looking intensely at his sketchpad, his hand sweeping away pink eraser flecks.

I take a deep breath and approach him. "So you work at Travis Elementary?" I say, seeing the logo on his shirt again.

"I was wondering when you were going to talk to me." He doesn't miss a pencil stroke. Who's he to make me speak first as if I were following him around?

"So what do you teach?" I say, feeling snippy. "Macaroni sculpture?"

He puts his pencil down and closes his eyes for a minute. "Sure," he sighs. "Macaroni sculpture and finger painting and Play-Doh pottery."

Two minutes. Two minutes of conversation and I'm already screwing things up. I hate the way he makes me act like a moody teen. I hate that he picks up his pencil, draws again, as if I weren't standing right next to him after all these years.

"So what are you doing?" I say.

"Getting ideas."

He offers his sketchpad. I take it and flip through six pages of Selena. "You drew this much in thirty minutes? Without looking at the wall?"

He says, "All I need are its dimensions."

"But the lines," I say because I believe that painting walls is like burning images into wood.

He takes back his pad, looks me straight in the eyes this time. "You're about to tell me that the wall's lines are supposed to dictate what I draw. I remember your philosophy, Sofía."

"It's not a . . ."

"You're still reading too much into things. It's just a wall. A huge page of cement."

"But what if something's really there?" I insist.

"It wouldn't matter."

"Why not?"

"Because I'm going to paint Selena anyway. That's what your boss Pete wants. Her glittery bras and voluptuous ass and that's what I'm going to give him." He closes the sketchpad, swallows the last of his beer, studies me a moment, smiles in a way that makes me blush. "Come on," he says, standing up, "boogie conmigo."

When I don't answer, he looks away, stone still. A long band of muscle protrudes from beneath his jaw and frames a deep depression at the base of his neck. He's heavy in a mild weight-lifting way, his hands large, their veins running the length of his forearms and disappearing beneath his sleeves. He runs a hand through his short, loosely curled hair, his face superbly calm.

"Come on," Susie yells across the restaurant. She and Frank are already walking toward the floor. "Don't make us dance alone."

"OK," I say, more to David than to her.

We're tentative at first, awkward, but soon I find the one-two-three of David's steps, sense his hand's slight pressure before he spins me beneath his arm. Susie and Frank are spinning too, Frank's wide smile and silver tooth catching the neon light and throwing it back at me. I catch a glance held too long between Parker at the jukebox and César at the bar before my vision blurs in the wild turning. The crescent streaks from our shoes on the floor mark our feet's movement as we dance below the feeble glow of yellow light flickering to the pulse of the wavering vibrato— "Beatriz, Marta, Isabel."

"¿Dónde está mi Chimuelita?" Pete calls, and she appears with her breasts hanging low, her floured arms, her leather chanclas flip-flopping. La Sandía Queen and her red chicken man show us how it's really done, weave their bodies into elaborate knots, gracefully untie themselves, their bodies spinning and circling each other with a rhythm and a constancy that can only be compared to the planetary orbits of the universe.

CHAPTER 3

The Susie Way

I like to steam up the bathroom before I shower, and when the mirror fogs up, my face seems a faint impression of myself that frightens me a bit—the indistinctness, the lack of detail— like a sketch partly rubbed away. Looking in the mirror, I see that my shoulders are too bony, not the kind of shoulders a person can lean on. I feel like a screen sometimes because of the cool air or heat rushing through me. Like with the woman at the flea market, I can sometimes see through people or buildings, through their porous sheet rock and skin, revealing everything's medieval two-dimensionality. Seems like the only things I can't see through are Pete, Chimuelita, and wood.

Yesterday Susie told me to dress up when applying for the mortgage loan, and in my conservative dress, I feel like a woman going on an interview, my stomach knotted with nerves, my panty-hose tight around my legs, my feet like a ballerina's in their heels. I dress the way Susie might in the same situation, making my lips and eyes the color and shape of lips and eyes in magazines. I should be holding some product—hairspray, a diet Coke, tampons.

The cars at the bank are carefully parked within the white lines, shrubs are clipped to sharp-edged squares, and a gray metal sculpture twists upward like a helix of DNA. The fountain has no

33

mildewed rim, no make-a-wish pennies, no fallen leaves, no droplets straying outside the pool. I stare into it, but the heavy chlorine smell makes me nauseous. Mirrored glass walls stand before and behind me so that I see my approach but also the reflection of my leaving. In the panes lies a whole panorama of flashing streetlights and streaming cars topped by a thin band of sky, a moving scene that makes the glass seem to bloat up, then implode. Here's a mural that steals its images from the street, inverting and then hurling them back to the opposite side, its colors shooting through me back and forth between the panes.

Before I can leave my oily fingertips on the front door's glass, it opens automatically. I clunk-clunk to a single-file line. Unlike the flea market where clots of people push through the aisles, we stand like a taut rope, no one swaying or peeking over shoulders, and I don't see the face of the dark-haired man before me or learn the age of the breath from behind.

I aimed for the businesswoman look and tied my hair in a tight bun, but the few strands whipping my neck feel conspicuously heavy. I thought I did everything right, the Susie way—my heels, my makeup, my pantyhose exactly parallel to my toes. What did I expect? I'm not a businesswoman, but a waitress and a flea market clerk fighting against the urge to sneeze.

"How may I help you?" the teller behind the counter says, her fingers poised above the keyboard, ready to type my name.

"I'm here for a loan."

"You have the wrong floor," she says, almost scolding. "Go upstairs."

At the second floor I sign my name in the guest book and wait for one of the loan officers sitting in a large room of cubicles separated by glass panes, their ears on the phones and eyes on computer screens. The men wear white shirts and dark silk ties, and the women wear white shirts and dark linen skirts, all of them multiplied in the reflective glass with their leather attachés and watches which are probably synchronized each day after they say the "Pledge of Allegiance," hands over hearts, eyes reverently gazing at the cans on their desks where the red, white, and blue flags hang limply on their dowel rod stems like weak flowers. I hear their chairs' soft scooting and their printers and their rapidly typing fingers. They whisper and their voices sweep past me like ghosts.

A man calls my name and I follow him through the cubicle maze to his desk.

"What kind of loan?" he asks.

"A mortgage loan."

He gives me an application and a clipboard with a pen. "Fill that out. Be sure to print."

I look at it. "Uniform Residential Loan Application," its questions numbered like a quiz: *borrower's name, social security number, home phone, employer, job title, gross monthly income, and monthly housing expenses.* All easy questions, but then I get to *Are you presently delinquent or in default on any Federal debt or any other loan, mortgage, financial obligation, bond, or loan guarantee?* My throat tightens because of my history with MasterCard.

It was all Susie's idea. She came back from San Antonio full of financial advice, said I needed to establish a credit history, and handed me an application that was already completed except for my signature. When I got my card in the mail, I waved it like a magic wand and bought useless things like perfumed soaps, a silver anklet, throw pillows, socks, and ten-dollar-a-pound chocolates from the Godiva store. I reached my credit limit in less than a week and relished my packages—the boxes lined in white tissue that enveloped my purchases like shawls around soft babes, the gift bags with Victorian floral prints and braided handles, the satin ribbons tied around my new underwear. I left the packages strewn about the house in a purposely careless way and showed them off, matter-of-factly, when visitors came by. But soon the colors faded and small lizards burrowed into them, and I realized that despite their prettiness, they were mere trash no different from emptied cereal boxes or cartons of saltines. I crumpled them, threw them away, and put my MasterCard in a shoebox full of recipes.

I wasn't timely in repaying my bill and MasterCard became synonymous with mean letters and scolding telephone calls. Knowing I'm already screwed, I mark the "no" box for being delinquent on my bills. I think I can get away with this little lie, but then my pen runs across the application as if the ink has discovered its own will. I wipe it with a tissue from my purse, but it smears, dark and viscous like old blood. This isn't like writing with fire, which is clean and only a matter of pressure and stroke, which can be controlled with an on/off switch.

I finally complete the form, but there's one thing missing. "Where do I put how long I've lived there?" I ask.

"How long you've lived where?" the loan officer says.

"In the house I want to buy because I've been there for thirty years. Renting."

"Renting?" He peers over the rim of his glasses. "Then it isn't technically yours?"

"No, not technically, but I've lived there all my life." He adjusts his glasses apathetically and gives a heard-it-all-before sigh. I don't get it. The bank wants every other fact about me—my marriage status, my ethnicity, my gender, my age, whether or not I served in the military—but where I've been living doesn't matter. I thought I could get extra points for living in the house I want to buy. I might have screwed up my credit card, but I've never been late with the rent.

"You could ask my landlord, Mr. Vela," I say. "He wants me to buy the house."

"I'm sorry, Miss Sauceda, but how long you've lived there is irrelevant."

He starts mumbling a little speech about interest rates and escrow accounts. I try paying attention but these are just words, the signs of indeterminate things. When I look at him, I see my own rouged and lipsticked face bouncing back at me from his lenses.

"You should have our decision within three to four weeks."

"Your decision?"

"The bank's."

"But who's in charge? I'd like to talk to him. Explain my situation."

"It's no one person," he says, getting impatient. "Besides, the only explanation we need is your income and your credit history."

He takes my application, inputs the data. I begin to see through the pale beige computer, the currents of electricity running through it, the binary pathways like a railroad with open and closed switch points, my facts reduced to zeros and ones. I understand that my fate isn't a matter of God's intervention but of mathematics. He punches the Return key, my information flashes off, and I imagine a slight bulge in the cables as my data shoots through.

When I exit the bank, I see a security guard shooing away an old begging woman.

"Los pobrecitos," Chimuelita often says about street people.

"Show them any kindness," Pete yells back, "and they'll keep coming 'round like stray dogs!" I've seen him, though, giving away leftovers, change, and a smile every now and then.

"Please, child," the woman says from the street corner, off bank property. She reaches out, palm up, grit between the creases of her fingers. She wears several layers of dirty clothes and a hat that half covers her face. "Nothing, see?" the hurried people say.

"I've got money," I say, running up to her. After all, what was her evil? What does she want but what we all want? Faith, hope, money. I remember fables with kings, queens, or gods disguised in beggar's garments, their opulent rewards for those who welcomed them despite their haggard looks. I put some quarters in the old lady's hand, but nothing happens. No grand transformation. She puts the change in a dirty sock, walks away, and even when the shadows down the street overcome her and she turns that last corner, she's still an old woman from the streets. Why do I pretend with myself? It isn't charity that makes me spare the change. It's a greed, a deep greed for magic. *Please child, please child, please . . .*

I'm still thinking of the old woman and those fables when I turn into a gas station where I see the promising scratch-off lottery cards—Gold Fever, Sunny Money, Piñata Payout, Break the Bank. The most they offer is ten thousand.

"Give me five quick picks," I say to the cashier. Maybe I can win the four-million-dollar prize.

I'm almost asleep when Julián raps on the door. I let him in, and he gives me a tattered romance novel, a wounded Union soldier in the arms of a nurse who almost looks like Florence Nightingale except for the deep cleavage.

"I'm too old to be your girlfriend," I say, taking the novel anyway. He brings me things all the time—pan dulce, hair barrettes, flowers from some old woman's garden—whatever he can afford with his allowance or take from his mother's shelves.

I serve him some tea, take a lemon wedge and squeeze its juices in the glass. A seed falls in and settles beneath the ice. Julián drinks in loud, thirsty gulps, his eyes closed as he savors the ice melting on his tongue.

"You think you can get me a job at Pete's?" he asks.

"Why?"

"I need money."

I tell him not to hurry. "Why rush into the real world?" I ask, remembering my experience at the bank.

"Well what world am I in now?" he asks. "The fake one?"

I know he's old enough to have a job, but he seems too young. He's still in high school taking math and history classes and dressing for P.E., his mother still washes and folds his clothes, he still spends Saturdays practicing spin kicks with his friends or lying half-asleep while listening to cartoons. He probably doesn't know who the president is. If he works at Pete's, he'll be a busboy wearing a white T-shirt, an apron, and a silly paper hat. He'll roll a cart of dirty soap water, pick up plates of smeared rice and beans, wipe the counters with a musty rag, and sweep up paper towels and crumbs. He'll stoop over tables like an old man, his arms thickening as he lifts the heavy bins.

"At least talk to Pete," he says.

But I don't want to talk to Pete. I've had a frustrating day already and I want to forget work, forget Mr. Vela's plans, forget David's Selena.

"Let's go to the park," I say.

"Don't you have to go to work soon?"

"I can take the day off."

"But shouldn't you call in first?"

"Pete doesn't mind," I say. "I do it all the time."

We drive down Ayers. Around sunset, the cholos loiter around the parking lots with their Camaros and vintage pickups and long Buicks from the seventies. They sit on the hoods, their tattooed arms locked around their girlfriends' waists, revving their engines and occasionally squealing into the street. I see shadows in the alleys, tagging gang names or peeing on the walls. Julián straightens up, hangs his arm out the window, nods his head to the rap from someone's blaring radio. I speed up, take us past Pete's, past the Holiday Inn to Cole Park.

I can smell the salty ocean and hear the seagulls and the flap of sails, kites, picnic blankets, and towels of children drying off. Something about the Gulf, its wind or its wide expanse of water, makes me crave freedom. I take off my shoes, my feet soothed by the cool grass. It's almost night. Fishermen walk toward the pier with lanterns and ice chests full of bait and beer, shrimp boats return with their entourage of gulls, windsurfers fold up their sails, and lovers cautiously emerge to claim their benches.

In the park lies a concrete amphitheater that's used for community events like symphonies, political rallies, health fairs, or nondenominational prayer meetings. Sometimes people protest tax proposals or abortions here, hold karate or cosmetic surgery seminars, or demonstrate Soloflex machines, Hoover vacuums, or Jacuzzis. The building itself isn't owned and advertises no opinions, its concrete walls somehow managing to remain pristinely white.

"Let's go to the playground," Julián says. "Want to?" he adds like a nine-year-old.

We run to the slide still hot from the day, to the swings, my tongue feeling a sudden heaviness as I ascend. When I reach the peak, I let go and feel the ease and elation of flight like a toddler thrown in the air by a strong-armed father, confident that this father will set her down gently when the playing's done. Julián falls on the grass beside me, and we watch the city's street lamps turn on, the fishermen's vague silhouettes, and the sidewalk of moonlight on the sea. We sit in the grass for a long time, the chiggers alive around us. Julián plucks grassy blades from my hair and I pretend not to notice.

I thought we had settled things, but when we get to the house, he asks me about Pete's again.

"Why do you want to work there?" I say.

"I need money to buy things."

"Like what?"

"Just things," he shrugs.

I go to my Maxwell House Coffee can, a blue metal stump in a rectangle of light from the window. Why should he grow up so fast? I'd like him to remain green like a new shoot of wood, like a stem before its rings. I lift the coffee can's lid and take out a wad of bills.

"Here," I say, handing him the money. He counts it, stuffs it in his pocket, and I see the bulge there on his upper thigh where the dollars are.

4

Bayfest

I t's the end of October, so I'm not surprised when Mr. Vela raps
on the door to collect his monthly rent check. He wears the
same guayabera, Wranglers, and boots, has the same dent in
his hair when he removes his cowboy hat, but his voice has
changed, no softness or harshness in its tone, just a cool neutrali-
ty that communicates nothing beneath the words.

"I'll get the rent," I say, realizing that for the past thirty years
the rent checks have probably paid his mortgage and then some. He
stands uncomfortably on the porch like a salesman who has
knocked at an inconvenient time. He accepts the rent with apologetic eyes, puts it in his pocket without reading the sloppy numerals
on the check.

"I'm sorry about the whole deal," he says staring at his boots.

"Well, don't worry," I tell him. "I've already taken care of
things." I say this as if it's a real bother, like I had to give up eating and drinking and breathing to work out a deal.

He looks up finally and says, "Good, because I'd hate to leave
it to a stranger." I would have believed him a few weeks ago, but I
can't tell the truth anymore. Is he speaking sincerely or is he repeating by rote a mindless phrase of courtesy? I look beyond Mr. Vela
at the house across the street, its sidewalk and door directly across

from mine, its two front windows mirroring mine except that mine are missing half their shutters. My house might once have been as white as theirs, but Mr. Vela has long neglected the paint.

I search his face for some hint of our past. I was nine or ten when Hurricane Allen came, and Mr. Vela boarded up our windows, filled our tub and ice chests with water, restocked our batteries, gave us canned food, and begged us to stay with his family because he didn't trust the walls, said that he'd never forgive himself if we were injured. When my mother refused to leave, he offered to stay. His wife had their son, he explained, but we had no one—no man anyway—except for him.

I was afraid. Since my mother wouldn't take me to church, I invented one for myself, dusting and arranging the religious statues she hid beneath the sink in a box next to jars of used grease and roach spray. I constructed a makeshift altar, placed the statues, a rosary, a lithograph of Christ, and scented candles on a small coffee table. I knelt before it and uttered prayers against the storm.

"Where do you get these ideas?" my mother said, half scolding.

Then there was a false night, horizontal rain, and lightning like a skeletal hand scurrying across the sky. When we lost the electricity, all we had were the eerie orange flames of my candles hurling our tortuous shadows against the wall. I heard crashing glass, buzzing electrical wires, splintering trees, and a wailing wind, but in front of all this noisy chaos was my shrine. What could I do but lie on my blankets, curl into a tight pill-bug ball, and sleep?

After the storm, telephone wires lay limp on the ground, the fence's wooden planks were scattered like a dropped box of toothpicks, and a Huff's Foodtown sign with a jalapeño man littered our front yard. Mr. Vela danced, cheered, patted the house's walls the way a man would pat his wife's behind, my mother shook her head against his silliness, and I thanked the saints.

"She sure is stubborn," Mr. Vela said because he was proud of the house. He looked down the street at a house that had lost its roof and another that was leaning against a tree like a drunken man, but ours still stood.

How can he forget the hurricane and the way this house became an exoskeleton bracing itself against the wind, aching, probably, when assaulted by the shrapnel of windblown debris? How can he sell it as if it had no more life than an automobile or TV?

"I better go," Mr. Vela says when he sees Frank's truck parking at the curb. He tries avoiding Susie, but she's too quick, calling him over and asking about the house. She's a sight in a tightly fitted T-shirt and a flamboyant ballroom skirt with hoops and layers of tulle, a drab outfit that must have come from the Goodwill store. Her hair is an intentional mess, and her face only half-painted. An earring dangles without its partner. I join them at the curb, expecting to hear Susie's tirade, but no, they're discussing market values and the pros and cons of hiring a real estate agent. By the time Frank and Mr. Vela go to examine a strange noise in the truck's engine, I'm steaming mad.

"Whose side are you on?" I ask.

Susie laughs as if my anger is unwarranted. "I'm on your side. Didn't I tell you to get a mortgage loan? Didn't I say that Mr. Vela's doing you a favor?"

"A favor?"

"Sure. What if he has a heart attack? Who gets the house then?"

"He's not old enough to have a heart attack."

"How do you know? He's getting pretty worn looking to me."

"He's as healthy as he was twenty years ago," I say, defensive. Selling the house is one thing, but the thought of Mr. Vela dying or even getting worn-out old is inconceivable. There are certain verities of this world that must remain intact and Mr. Vela's health is one of them.

"Here comes your little boyfriend," Susie says, and when I turn around, Julián's bike screeches to a halt beside Frank's truck.

He doesn't waste a minute. "So you're throwing her out?" he says to Mr. Vela, straightening his shoulders and puffing his chest like an angry rooster.

Susie walks right up to him, says, "Aren't you a little musketeer?" Then she pinches his cheeks, a gesture that deflates his puffed-up rooster chest.

Mr. Vela shakes his head, puts on his cowboy hat, says, "Got to go," from beneath the shadow of his hat brim, and drives off.

There's a few silent seconds before I remember Susie's ridiculous costume. "Who are you supposed to be?" I ask.

"Cinderella."

"Cinderella?"

"You're only half-dressed," Julián says.

"That's because I'm Cinderella in transition."

I say, "The fairy godmother is just changing you into a princess?"

"No, I'm Cinderella at midnight. After she snags the prince, but while the spell is starting to wear off." She winks at Frank. "This used to be my carriage," she says, holding up the plastic pumpkin she's using as a purse.

"Show them your shoes," Frank says.

She lifts her hem. "Flip-flops. Tomorrow I'll get that glass slipper and it'll fit perfectly."

"And who are you supposed to be?" I ask Frank, who's in a white shirt and white slacks with a black marker hanging from a string around his neck.

"I'm a page," he says.

"A royal page?"

"No, just a page."

"Don't you get it?" Susie asks, but I shake my head. "Frank's a page like a blank page in a book. We're going to let people write on him. See?" She takes the marker and scribbles, *To be or not to be.*

"You're quoting Hamlet now?"

"What's Hamlet?" Julián asks. "That's a line from a perfume commercial."

Susie tousles his hair. "Can I take him home with me?" she teases, and I notice a diamond ring on her finger.

"You're engaged?" I ask as if it were a shameful thing. Why is she getting married? She can't actually love Frank. I see them snuggling before me with that phony premarital glow, looking more like puppy lovers than serious adults in their stupid costumes. Susie laughs, her mouth a wide-open gong. I stare into it, see her upper palate's ridges, her dark throat, her hollow lungs. *This isn't a game*, I feel like saying because she takes things so lightly, treats them as carelessly as a cat chasing Christmas tree balls. She hugs me, kisses me, leaves a cool Judas spot on my cheek. She takes Frank's marker again, writes *heart* on the wrong side of his chest.

"You're going to be my maid-of-honor, but we'll talk about it later," she says. "We're off to Bayfest now."

I watch Frank open his Chevy truck door, kiss her hand, and whisper sweet nothings in her ear. When they drive off, the exhaust dirties the air like a puff of dust from a horse's heels, the sky hot pink before them.

"You want to go too?" I ask, and Julián nods.

Bayfest is no more than a glorified bazaar that began in 1976 to celebrate the bicentennial, although selling arts and crafts and eating hot dogs has little to do with our country's birthday. It's too hot to celebrate in July, so the festival was moved to the last weekend of October. I guess it's a good way for the city to earn some extra cash. What began as a few vendors has ballooned to the point of bursting. Shoreline Drive between the Coliseum and Selena Auditorium is closed off, nearby businesses lock their doors and board up windows against the revelry, and police officers carry nightsticks just in case. There are too many food booths, tents, portable toilets, and people pushing against the fences and the seawall. Once in the crowd, we're helpless against its flow.

Julián and I see a green-faced, wart-nosed witch and a Snow White who's exchanged her dwarfed men for a robust Zorro bowing debonairly before ladies whistling, not at his reputed fame, but at his open fly and underpants starkly white against his black jeans. A fanged wolf in blue overalls carries a stuffed lamb, its leg gnawed off and coat streaked with curlicues of fake blood. Fairies drop glitter on us. A red man with a string of dead fish writes *Red Tide* on a sign because he doesn't want to be mistaken for the devil, whom we also see, his pitchfork playfully poking the asses of veiled harem girls, buxom mermaids, and gray-haired cheerleaders. Mickey Mouse cavorts with a barmaid in fishnet hose, Cleopatra fondles the Energizer Bunny's ears, and Romeo flirts with Betty Boop. We see Washington, Lincoln, and Kennedy holding up a stumbling Statue of Liberty with a roasted turkey leg for a sconce, and Elvises, Marilyn Monroes, and Selenas too numerous to count.

The crowd makes me nervous. "Let's look for an open space," I say, and Julián grips my sleeve, pulls me to an arcade with a mechanical wizard in a glass case, a Merlin with a purple robe of stars and crescent moons, a wand, an orb, a cone-shaped hat, and a white beard trimmed to a perfect V.

"Try it," he says, so I put a quarter in the slot. The orb lights up and a tiny speaker utters its abracadabra's. The wizard man nods, his eyes without pupils, his lip paint faded away. The machine spits out my fortune, which hangs there like a white tongue. Do Not Linger Too Long in Your Life's Spring, it says.

"What does that mean?" I ask.

"I don't know. It's the end of October already." Julián bangs the side. "Cheap thing," he says. We don't bother to explain my fortune. Like he said, it's a cheap trick—twenty-five cents for a senseless quote on a thin slip of paper.

Julián leads me through the crowd to a magician's booth, Señor Surprise with a little card table and a bag of tricks. "First one's free. The rest a dollar," he says. "Pick a card, any card, pick the card that will love you best." Julián chooses one, secretly shows me an ace of spades. "Put it here," Señor says. Then he riffles the deck, cascades it, spreads it on the table so that all the cards face down but one, the ace of spades. We stand transfixed before the magician, put our dollars in his upturned sombrero, desperate for more. "Meet King Pepe and Queen Chula," he says, making the cards vanish only to reappear in Julián's pocket. Coins emerge from Señor's nostrils and ears, matches levitate, Barbie becomes Ken. For a while, we succumb to the magic. If I wave Señor's plastic wand, will dollars appear in my coffee can? Will Mr. Vela change his mind?

After Señor Surprise, we walk through booths of potters, knitters, sculptors, popsicle-stick architects and their buildings perfectly rendered with the wooden refuse of our Eskimo Pies. We follow a labyrinth of quilts suspended from clotheslines, their patterns fashioned after nature—pine tree, flying geese, maple leaf, honeybee. In the center is a huddle of black-robed witches hunched over a large frame, their bony, age-spotted hands puncturing fabric with bright metallic thread that glistens like brief sparks of fire.

"What pattern are you working on?" I ask.

"Crazy quilt," one says without missing a stitch.

"What's it supposed to look like?"

"Nothing," another answers, quilting a collage of odd-shaped remnants. I stare at their quilt, its design as confused as the motley crowd outside. I try to make sense of it, but the moment a shape begins to emerge from the dissonant sulfur and brake-light red—a phoenix or spike-backed cat—Julián calls me, his voice making the vague shape disappear.

"It's you," he says, leading me to a caricature at another booth.

"That's not me," I say, in spite of the figure's pyroelectric pen, small like a toothpick or twig.

"You like it?" I look up and there's David unplucking the caricature from a corkboard and offering it to me. I wave it away.

"You drew that?" I say, indignant.

"Sure. So people could see what I do."

"For advertising, you mean?"

"I didn't think you'd mind." There's a long line of people waiting to be ridiculed by his chalk. He's got a cigar box full of dollar bills.

"Isn't Pete's restaurant enough?" I say. "Don't you have a regular job too?"

"What's wrong with making a little money on the side?"

"You want me to buy it?" Julián asks, taking out some change to pay David, who seems so eager to make a transaction of my face.

I'm about to wad up the picture when I hear Susie calling my name. I turn around and see her fake tiara. "Check out Frank," she says, and he turns slowly, a breathing page of graffiti. WIDE LOAD on his ass. FOR THE KINGDOM, THE POWER, AND THE GLORY ARE YOURS and VERONICA'S A BITCH on his thighs. I THINK, THEREFORE, I AM smudged on his oily forehead. COCA COLA IT'S THE REAL THING, McDonald's golden arches, Starkist Charlie, the Chevrolet cross. "Here," Susie says, handing me the marker. "Write something." Frank's surface waits, but I can't do it, can't add to that mess. Julián takes the pen, writes *Julián con Sofía* inside a big lopsided heart.

"How cute," Susie laughs.

My face doesn't belong on David's paper and my name doesn't belong on Frank's shirt. There's no depth to paper, no grain, and cotton disintegrates if it's washed with too much bleach. It's the impermanence that bothers me. Everyone stands in a tight, mocking ring around me and I feel trapped—trapped by David's chalk, by Julián's lopsided heart, by Susie's flitty laughter, by everyone trying to place my face and name where they don't belong.

I leave them, pushing my way past La Llorona, Artemis, Eve. I hit a wall of arm-linked men in Dolly Parton attire—blond wigs, sequins, beach-ball tits. "Come to my theme park," one says, putting his hand to his crotch. A Crayola box, a Bud Light can, a carton of Whoppers walk around me on their sticklike human legs. I'm stuck in a mesh of arms, people pressing against me like slow-motion schools of fish unconsciously shifting back and forth. All I see are 'huge laughing nostrils and beer bellies. Everywhere an armpit-and-popcorn scent. Before us children dance on a stage in ballet folklórico costumes—colorful but hot with petticoats and sleeves. The girls' lashes mascara-thick and hair in tight, ribboned braids. Sometimes I think love should be as clean and uncomplicated as those dancers—not sweaty like my mother's or frivolous like Susie's. The drunk couples around me grab each other's asses, grope each other's tongues, and wipe glistening spit from their chins, but the girls on the stage stomp and whirl their skirts to "Jalisco's" festive notes and snub the little boys who circle them, their hats clutched behind their backs. No one holds hands. It's all very genteel.

For a moment the dance soothes me, but then I see David pushing his way through the crowd. I try disappearing, but he grabs my elbow.

"Where are you going?" he asks.

"I'm trying to find my way out of this crazy place."

His face softens, gets a concerned, apologetic look. "I'm sorry about the picture," he says. "I tore it up if that makes you feel better."

"You didn't give it to Julián?"

He shakes his head. He's got an honest face, and as I stare into it, the world seems to slow down. Here in the midst of all these mythical and pop culture beasts, a pocket of privacy envelops us and mutes the wild noise of Bayfest, creating an intimate silence that shatters when I hear Julián calling my name and see him waving from the hood of a parked truck.

"You better set that kid straight, 'cause he's got a big crush on you."

"He's harmless," I say.

I think it's funny. I laugh in a Susie way, which gets David mad. "You think it's some kind of game hanging around with a boy like that?"

"He's not a boy," I say, still laughing.

"What's the matter with you?" David looks as if he'd like to shake some sense into me. "You should be out on a real date, Sofía. Dancing or watching a movie instead of eating cotton candy with a sixteen-year-old."

I don't like his patronizing voice. "Who are you to tell me what to do? It's not like we've got something between us."

He just throws up his hands, tells me to forget it, and walks away. I find myself hoping he'll turn back, but when he doesn't, I feel like punishing him somehow, so when Julián finds me, I ask him if he wants to get married. "There's a booth over there," I say, pointing to a mock wedding booth sponsored by a science fiction club. He laughs when he sees it. It's such a corny, adolescent thing to do, but we run to it anyway.

When we get there, robots, aliens, and three-eyed monsters from movies or TV shows greet us. The booth has a gray, futuristic church spire topped not by a cross, but by a V-shaped antenna. At the entrance is a statue made of smooth, reflective tin-can skin—a metal barrel for a torso, strings of vegetable cans for arms and legs, a wire-hanger halo, cellophane wings. I guess it's an angel or the science fiction version of a deity.

Julián and I can get married for a mere three dollars. We pay. We go inside where a Martian clips a plastic bow tie on Julián's collar and gives me a lacy tablecloth veil and a Venus flytrap in a terra cotta pot for a bridal bouquet. We hear an electric guitar's wedding march. Then a bald woman in a white robe tells us to repeat after her, but instead of the traditional "till death do us part," she speaks pure nonsense. But what are words anyway? What's David's apology or Mr. Vela's hope that I'll buy the house? Most of the time, words are nothing but veils blinding truth—not like sounds, which are the truths themselves, a buzz, a ring, a yelp. We repeat after her, laughing the whole time, even when Julián

49

gives me a cheap ring that can be squeezed or opened to fit my finger. A computer prints out our names and our "joined in holy matrimony."

"Can I drive your car?" Julián asks when we join the crowd again. "I have my permit now." He pulls his permit from his pocket. I look at the smooth, inexperienced skin of his cheeks and temples, his lack of stubble and scars. He shouldn't be driving yet. He should be shooting basketball or playing Monopoly, Yahtzee, or Mortal Kombat. "Until I take my road test, I can only drive with someone over eighteen."

My Suburban's rusted. It's got a rattling muffler and a crooked antenna that picks up only stations on the AM radio dial—conjuntos, country, news. I keep a lot of junk in it—old blankets, an umbrella, an extra coat, a stew pot from Pete's. It's also very big. I've got to climb a step to get into it and sit up straight to see over the steering wheel. "You don't want to drive my ugly car," I say.

"Please." He uses a different voice when he wants something, a softer voice that almost betrays his tenacity. "Only for a little while."

What bothers me most is that he'll choose a destination and he may or may not tell me what it is. I give in anyway, toss my keys to him. When he starts the engine, he's very confident and proud of those mundane movements that make a car go—the parking brake's release, the shift into drive, the glances in the rearview mirror. He's showing off, and by the time we've left the parking lot, he has rolled down the window and put his arm on the door.

As I watch that bloated pride across his face, I realize that this drive is part of America's lame rite of passage, an initiation into cars and everything that goes with cars—sex and drinking binges and exhilarating speed. Even Mr. Vela hopes to drive a mythic journey across the country like a contemporary Odysseus defeating the virtual beasts of America's theme parks in a cross-country loop back to home. Here I am, the over-eighteen chaperone symbolically holding Julián's hand. There's nothing ceremonial about this drive down a street crowded with fruit stands, muffler shops, and banks. Julián fidgets with the radio dial, but the sky's silent tonight. In the ancient days, it would have spoken with thunder or a light wind, and I would have been the priestess that blessed his kill instead of this anxious pair of eyes double-checking the blind spot before he changes lanes.

He parks along a strip of beach at Padre Balli Park.

In Corpus Christi, if I face the water and tilt my head to catch the full volume of wind and waves, I can forget that I live in a city and everything that goes with cities—boundaries and papers that give a person legal rights to property. Ever since Mr. Vela decided to sell the house, I've hated fence lines and street lines and loved only the lines in wood and the horizon's hairline beyond reach.

There's the crescent moon's sliver of light and a crane standing on the ocean. I once thought my mother could stand on the ocean too. She would swim, and when she reached a certain point, she would stand and the bay's brown sludge would seem solid at her feet.

"How did you do that?" I asked her once.

"I'll show you."

Maybe I was seven or eight years old. I held my mother's shoulders and she swam easily, too light for sinking, floating even with my added weight and the currents fighting beneath her. The sea's swells always broke behind us. I saw the bobbing cloverleafs of dozens of medusas passively riding the water, their tentacles sparing us. The salt water left a dryness in my mouth and stung my eyes, but my mother was unaffected because she belonged here somehow. She opened her eyes under water and they never reddened, swallowed its saltiness without getting thirsty.

She stopped swimming after a while. "Stand up," she said, and when I did, only my ankles were beneath the sea.

"How could we be so far?" I asked.

"We're on a sandbar," she said. "It's shallow here."

I felt disappointed. I liked having a mother who could walk on water, who could rise to sainthood that way. Still, we were at a precipice. The sandbar wasn't very wide, and beyond its shallow brown was the deep blue-black of a fathomless sea. Our toes dangled over this great height, and there was no way to fall.

"Look," Julián says, pointing to the dunes lightened by the city's hazy orange glow. He whispers, "Jackrabbits." I see dozens of rabbits perched on their haunches, their ears attentive to all sounds and silences, some hopping a few paces, others feeding on grass, a few keeping constant watch. They're beautiful, silhouetted atop the dunes like stenciled borders on a nursery's walls. "Let's try to catch one," he says. We run off, our steps sinking in the soft ground, the rabbits dispersing. We find a grassless bed of sand and rest there, breathing hard from all our running.

"The moon," he says, "looks like half a halo on your head."

I find myself desperately wanting to believe the myths of this world—Señor Surprise's sleights of hand, Susie's love for Frank, Chimuelita's stories, the magic money in my coffee can, and the dancers' clean expression of love. So when Julián tries to kiss me, I let him. It's the most perfect kiss—his lips as reverent on my cheek as a subject's on a sovereign's hand.

We sit quietly for a long time. The rabbits appear again, pawing the ground, disregarding us because we have rubbed off the scent of Corpus Christi. When we stand up, I see the depression where our bodies were, an inscription like lovers' names carved on trees. I glance back before we descend the dune, and a gust of wind fills the hollow with sand, leveling it again.

CHAPTER 5

Bésame

I gave David the silent treatment that week after Bayfest, but he ignored it.

"When are you going to look at my wall?" he asked.

"I'm not. I'm too busy working." He looked at the way I dawdled over an already polished counter and walked off when I didn't change my mind.

"You don't know anything about men," Chimuelita scolded. "Take a break and go outside like he asked."

I tried telling her to quit playing matchmaker, but she ordered Parker to cover my tables and urged me out the door before I could muster the words. I reluctantly went to the side of Pete's restaurant where David sat on a wooden crate mixing a gallon of white paint. He heard me turn the corner but he didn't look up.

"What did you want me to see?" I asked.

"Nothing. I just hoped we could talk."

"About what?"

"About whatever."

"You called me out here to talk about whatever?" I asked as if speaking to an impertinent child.

He stopped mixing and stood up. "Will you get over it, Sofía?"

"Over what?"

"That stupid picture I drew. How many times do I need to apologize?" I wanted to say he was crazy for thinking I could hold a grudge so long, but he was right. I felt like he was ridiculing my woodburning when I saw that picture. He said, "You can do one of two things—remember forever or forget."

I considered it. I saw his forearms speckled with paint, his neck mildly sunburned, and the way his reserved frustration made him tap his foot. He looked back at me, penetratingly, and I found myself drawn to his eyes, his hair and ears temptingly soft.

"I guess I could forget," I said.

He half smiled and squinted. His foot slowed down. "I guess I could forget too, then."

"Forget what?"

"The million times you hurt my feelings."

I felt embarrassed. He has this way of turning me into an adolescent. When he said this, I imagined my behavior like a chart full of demerits. "I don't know what gets into me," I said, trying to apologize.

He sat on the crate again and returned to mixing paint. "It takes too much effort staying mad, Sofía."

I lingered a while longer, but we didn't speak. A sudden shyness overcame us and we couldn't work our way around it. We've hardly spoken since, though there's a truce between us. David probably would have finished Pete's wall sooner, but he took frequent breaks in the restaurant where he usually stared at me and made me feel like glass the way he continued to speak to Pete, uninterrupted, as if his eyes weren't steadfast on me.

Today he's taken down his scaffold and draped a large white tarpaulin over his work, and I find myself curious to see it. There's a parking lot full of people waiting to view the wall—a reporter from the *Corpus Christi Caller Times*, Pete and Chimuelita, their sons with their wives and children, and Chimuelita's sister, known to everyone as Tía Lupe. Pete's family greets the guests, and I recognize their characteristic smile and a confidence in their shoulders.

Pete speaks to the reporter. "Next to the day I met my beautiful wife and the birth of my four sons and when they got married and had all my grandchildren and when I met my friends—next to all that, this is the proudest day of my life."

But it isn't really Pete the reporter wants to speak to. This is David's wall now. He's donned an outfit of starving-artist black and a hoop earring. It's silly the way girls giggle around him like he's a celebrity, the way they notice his hands, strong and brown with plump veins just beneath the skin and soft tufts on his knuckles.

"I didn't want to capture Selena," he says, "but the essence of her." He stands against the wall for a picture, his black outfit stark against the white drape. The photographer looks through his lens, counts to three, blinds us with a bright flash. David says, "Should I take another? Just in case?" He poses again, this time showing us his profile. I can't stand his ease and his Susie-style flirtation with the crowd. I'm ready to go inside, but the tarpaulin drops and before the fabric settles on the ground, the people clap and cheer, impressed by his work. "How lifelike," I hear them say. They can hardly wait to shake his hand, get his autograph on their paper towels or receipts, go inside for a cheap meal or a beer.

So there she is, Selena, two stories high. David has painted many coats over the sun behind La Virgen and over her steadfast-ly opened eyes, but a bit of color has seeped through anyway. He's walked into the restaurant speckled with paint, his hair wrapped in a bandana, his shoulders slightly drooped. "She's so stubborn!" We've heard him exclaim, "¡La Virgen que no quiere dormir!" He's managed merely a Selena pasted upon La Virgen's form. The yellow sunbeams are now spotlights. The blue of La Virgen's cape is now a stage curtain's blue. Where the angels were, he has paint-ed adoring fans. Braids encircle Selena's head like a crown, and her eyes bore into us beneath thick wingspan brows. There's the sequined bra, hip-hugging pants, and platform shoes standing, not on the moon, but on the gold bell of her Grammy Award. I can still see, in a certain angle of sun, the eyes of baby Jesus peeping through the gramophone beneath her feet.

David pushes through the crowd. "What do you think?" he asks.

"Still looks like La Virgen to me," I say, unimpressed.

"And why shouldn't she?" he says. "The only real difference is the costume."

But what about the mystery? I think. Selena isn't mysterious—not even in her meticulously televised death. She's nothing like La

Virgen appearing before Juan Diego, giving him roses on that cold December day and her image on his tilma, a concrete sign for the doubting bishop, who must have gone home wondering why she would choose to reveal herself to a lowly Indian and not to him, Bishop Zumárraga, man of God. I've met people who've made the pilgrimage to Mexico to see the tilma. Maybe I'll see it someday too and maybe something miraculous will happen, a convulsion of faith because the tilma remains mysterious despite the scientists' analyses and microscopes. This is why we see La Virgen in the grutas, in the shrines, in old ladies' homes, and in the gold medallions hanging from neck chains and on T-shirts too. I once saw a man walking shirtless on the beach, a Virgin tattoo spanning the whole length of his back. But then, I've seen Selena tattoos too and shrines made in her honor. Maybe she wouldn't be a near deity today if she hadn't died so young, before the natural disinterest that eventually subdues all fans. She might have avoided this mass marketing of her name, face, and private life.

After a while, everyone goes inside to eat. David sits at the corner, signs a few more autographs and shakes a few more hands, but the crowd doesn't find him as interesting as the beer and food. I walk sideways and carry the trays high to get through the crowded tables. My apron soon gets heavy with tips. Pete has to send his grandchildren upstairs so his sons and daughters can be waiters and cooks. Parker and César share a rhythm behind the bar, a language that shifts privately between them and reminds me of the way Julián and his friends paint walls—that wonderful lack of hesitation. I wish I shared that with someone too.

"I bet you've never made this much money," I tell Pete.

"Not in one night, Sofía. Not in one night." He gets a thoughtful squint in his eyes and looks up at the ceiling. He says, "Let's close early tonight. As soon as these people finish eating, let's lock the doors and have our own party."

He puts a Closed sign in the window. When the last customer leaves, he shouts out, "¡Cervezas pa' todos!" His sons bring in ice chests full of beer, toss our drinks to us, our hands cupped for the cold, wet thuds of cans gently arcing through the air. One slips through David's fingers. He picks it up, rubs it across his forehead, then takes a towel and wipes the moisture away. Pull-tabs pop and the soft fizz seeps over. Pete toasts his family and friends. "Like primos," he says to Parker and me, "and you'll always be welcome in our home." We drink nothing but bubbles at first, but when the fizz settles, the beer goes down as easily as water or tea. The aluminum cans sparkle in the light. We crush them afterwards, pile them against the wall. In their crumpled state, they look like wadded paper or shiny dollar bills.

"Chimuelita," Pete calls.

"¿Qué quieres, viejo?"

"More beer, por favor."

"Sing," she says, "and I'll think about it."

"Hey good lookin', what ya got cookin'?" he sings in a gravelly voice. Chimuelita strokes his sideburns, plucks a red hair, makes a wish and blows it away while Pete rubs the sting from his cheek. "Ándale," he says, getting impatient. When she casually walks to the bar, Pete gazes at her wide behind's sway and Chimuelita somehow senses him, turns with a seductive wink and a flirtatious throwing of kisses. "¡Masota!" Pete utters, his shoulders quivering.

"¿Dónde está Tía Lupe?" Chimuelita calls when she returns, and everyone scoots aside as she makes her way through us. "Canta, por favor."

Tía Lupe emerges from a dark corner, a guitar already in her hands. Someone places a stool on the dance floor where she sits with a certain deliberateness that hushes us. She has a solid body, not a loose weight that folds over itself, but a firm bulge like a mango or pear. I've seen women like Tía Lupe in Gauguin's paintings, women whose breasts seem almost to drip milk, with muscular arms, calves, and toes, with dark skin and eyes that close upon smiling. The wonderful fullness. And here I am, too skinny, a hard knob on my shoulders and a pair of bony hands.

Tía Lupe strums once. The sound ripples against my skin. "Uno, dos, tres," she says as her hands flutter over the strings and are blurred by her quick beating the way bees' wings are blurred. Her feet, head, and shoulders also play the guitar, whose rhythm reaches out to me and gently sways my hips, then my shoulders and hands begin clapping to the staccato beat.

A mí, me gusta el pim pi ri rim pim pim,
Con la botella pam pa ra ram pam pam,
Con el pim pi ri rim pim pim,
Con el pam pa ra ram pam pam,
El que no beba vino
Será un animal, será un animal.

"¡Canta conmigo!" she calls, and we all join in.

Beber, beber, beber es un gran placer.
El agua es para bañarse
Y pa' las ranas que nadan bien.

Our beer cans fly like shooting stars, and when we drink, the fizz spills over our chins, dampens our shirts, leaves its stickiness on our mouths, necks, and fingers and makes the floor swirl, the walls pulse, and the ceiling dip down. Singing and beer hollow out my bones, and if I remove my apron with its heavy change, I'll rise to the ceiling like a ball of helium. Everyone feels it, our legs wavering like legs departing carnival rides. All the jokes are funny, and with this lightness running through my veins, even David's mural seems artistic.

He takes a seat beside me. "Having a good time?" he asks.

"Yes," I say, out of breath from singing.

Then he grabs my hand beneath the table, holds it on his knee, and I'm aware of nothing but his cuff tickling my wrist and my own fingers gripping his with a surprising tenacity. The music settles down and he suggests that we leave, his voice urgent and charged. I'm tempted at first, but I prefer the simplicity of secretly holding hands beneath the table. "Come on," he says, already pushing back his chair to go.

"I can't," I say. "I've got to talk to Chimuelita. It's important." I walk away before he can sweet-talk me into leaving, but when I get to her, I can't think of anything to say. I look back and he's still watching me. "Where did your sister learn to sing?" I finally ask, knowing this will drive her to a story.

"Singing can't be learned," she says. "It's a gift like my cooking." She laughs at this boast of hers, sits back, and breathes deeply to release the beer's silliness. "Tía Lupe was one of those children with sueños malos all the time. I told her not to eat so much before sleeping, but she never listened because I was the oldest and I bossed her around too much. There was a large window where we slept and outside was a fig tree and a lamp across the street. So our room was never dark. We liked to look at the fig tree's shadows on our wall. We liked to make shadows with our hands too. Barking dogs. Seagulls. Big gorilla heads. Anyway, Tía Lupe had a dream about running from animals. I woke her up, and she pushed me away like I was a beast. But when she opened her eyes, all she saw was the fig tree and its shadows, and for some reason, she thought she was still asleep. She started screaming. She said the leaves and branches looked like the claws of wildcats and the light like evil eyes. And I tried, but nothing could wake her because she was awake already. Ever have those confusions?"

"Sometimes," I say because even though my mother's dead, even though I've boxed her books and sent her clothes to Goodwill, I've imagined her standing at the closet doorway in her robe or sitting in that fold-up lawn chair outside, and there are certain things I can't get rid of—pictures, figurines, the dust from her rouge in her dresser's top drawer. When the ivy's leaves dry up and fall, I sweep them up and then water it profusely because she complained about things like uncared-for plants.

"I started screaming too," Chimuelita says, "till my parents turned on the lights."

"And Tía Lupe?"

"We had to shake her. She was still confused. She thought she was having a dream within a dream because she couldn't tell the difference between awake and asleep. She had los sustos real bad. Every time she tried to talk, her voice came out like a stutter, like an old car that wants to start but never turns over, you know? So we called la curandera and she came to our house."

"What did she do?"

"She brought her broom. She moved our bed to the middle of the room and told Tía Lupe to lie down. She swept all around saying prayers. She even swept the wall where the shadows were." I imagine this curandera with a broom handle splintered and scarred by long fingernails. "She was there for a long time staring down at my sister. When Tía Lupe woke up, she knew she was awake."

"But that doesn't explain her voice," I say with mild disappointment.

"Without los sustos," Chimuelita explains, "she could talk again, but what came first was a song from church, a Latin one. We didn't know why she was singing. La curandera nodded and smiled like this was a normal thing. And Tía Lupe hasn't stopped singing since. Or talking either, la pobrecita." Chimuelita laughs, gets lost in her silliness again.

I watch as the jukebox casts an ethereal glow around Tía Lupe, her eyes serenely shut, her mouth a pleasant O. Chimuelita locks her arms around Pete's waist.

"¡Una romántica!" she calls to her sister.

Tía Lupe takes a cloth to wipe the moisture from her hands and from the guitar's neck as if to slow its pulse. She sits motionless, closes her eyes, sinks into her most passionate depths, and searches for the chord at her belly's core. When she strums this time, I see how much a woman the guitar is, that it has breasts and hips and a wide, gaping navel, that its neck eagerly outstretches itself for her hands. Her singing courts it, entwines itself around the strumming till the guitar and voice become a single strand of sound.

Bésame, bésame mucho
Como si fuera esta noche la última vez.
Bésame, bésame mucho
Que tengo miedo a perderte, perderte después.

There's a part of me that longs to feel the kind of intensity that rises from Tía Lupe's belly, but another part of me that fights it, that resists the way her voice goose-pimples the undersides of my arms and lures my eyes to David, who looks firmly back at me. Why does he keep looking at me? Maybe it's because Tía Lupe's voice wills people together. Pete and Chimuelita tighten their embrace, their mesmerized sons wander through the room in search of their wives, and when Parker sees a strand loose in César's face, he gently and unabashedly brushes it aside.

"What's this?" Pete says almost to himself when he notices the shy smile on César's face. "What's this?" he yells, stopping the music. He walks over to the bar, his steps large and heavy, his face a contortion of anger, which I don't understand because Parker and César never hid their feelings very well. "You think my son is some kind of fag?" Pete says to Parker. "You think you can come into my bar, my home, and act fresh with my son in front of all his relatives?"

"¡Déjalos!" Chimuelita says. "It's no secret."

"What's no secret?" he says, turning to all of us who don't want to move or whisper or breathe. Pete's restraint is as flimsy as a house of cards. "Does every goddamn person know but me?" His temple's veins bulge. He clenches his brows and flares his nostrils when he breathes. "Is it true, César?" César looks down, and Pete asks again, his voice softer and faltering. "Is it true?" When César looks up, everything in his face confirms it. Pete closes his eyes and rubs his forehead. For a moment, I think he'll accept things, let his anger go and continue with the party, but then he sucks in his lungs' full volume. "You're fired!" he yells at Parker. "Get your ass out of here!"

"Hold up, Pete," Parker says, trying to calm him down. "Let's talk about this."

"Talk? What the fuck does that mean?" Pete balls up his hand. "¿Sabes qué?" he says. "Talk about this!" He strikes Parker in the face, his arm a violent whir that sends Parker stumbling backward and busts his nose. Parker wipes the blood with the back of his hand, spits, and leaves.

As soon as the door shuts behind him, César stands eye to eye with Pete. "Don't ever hurt Parker again," he says, sealing his words with a hard gaze and then grabbing his keys from behind the bar.

"What we have here is a moment of truth," Pete yells at him, "a fucking moment of truth!" César stops at the door but doesn't turn around. "You're the most rebellious son I got—never wanting to do things my way. But this—this is too much. You don't care about Parker. You're just trying to spite me for making you go to school, for making you study something decent so you can have a good life for yourself."

"This isn't about you, Dad, or school. It's about me and what I want."

"You don't know what you want! This is your family, César, and families always stay, but fags like Parker come and go." César

61

only shakes his head. "That bolillo is messing with your mind," Pete insists. "He's got you confused."

"I'm not confused," César says, putting his hand on the door's crossbar.

Pete yells out his ultimatum. "If you walk out, you walk out forever!"

César stands at the pinnacle of his moment of truth, his hesitancy evident in his tight shoulders and tensed neck, but he walks out anyway. Through the window we see him running down the street, calling Parker's name.

We stand frozen for a long time. There's only the dissonant clanking of the ceiling fans rotating, unbalanced on their stems. Pete looks around. "What the hell are you looking at!" he yells and we scamper off like roaches surprised by sudden light.

I grab my purse from the kitchen, and when I return to the bar, Pete's at a table with his face in his hands and Chimuelita's arms around his shoulders. Their shapes melt into each other and together they cast one shadow on the wall. As I sneak my way out the door, I hear Pete's soft crying, and then the door clicks shut behind me.

"How did you like that scene?" David says. He's sitting on a bus bench outside the restaurant.

"What are you still doing here?" I ask.

"Waiting for you."

"Why?"

"Because tonight's the last time I'll have an excuse to see you and I'd like to know if it's OK to come back."

"You don't need my permission."

"Sure I do. If I come back, it's not to eat Chimuelita's food or talk to Pete, but to see you."

"What for?" I tease. "You hardly ever talk to me."

"Well you aren't easy to talk to. You like picking fights with me."

"I do not."

"Sure you do. You were ready to fight me about my mural earlier." He picks up a beer tab and flicks it across the street. "Well?"

"Well what?"

"You mind if I come by sometime?"

"I don't know," I say.

He leans forward, puts his elbows on his knees and his head in his hands. "What is it, Sofía? You hate me or something?"

"No, I don't hate you."

"Then what?"

I can't help being suspicious. "What do you really want?" I ask.

"I told you already. Maybe I could come by and visit you or just watch you work if you're too busy."

"Watch me work?"

"Why not? I like watching you. You're charmingly clumsy."

"I'm not clumsy," I snap back.

"Sure you are," he says as if being clumsy were my most endcaring quality.

I realize he's asking how I feel, and I'm caught between missing our old friendship and fearing the temptation of his eyes that stare, unashamed and unmindful of everything else around us. If I'm clumsy, it's because I'm working beneath his steadfast gaze, which acts like a trip wire at my feet. I resent having to betray myself, the way he's put our future in my hands. For a long time, I teeter with uncertainty as he calmly waits for an answer. When he finally looks up, I want to utter poetry, but all I can say is, "I wouldn't mind if you came by."

When I turn the corner, I see the TV's blue-gray light blinking through my house's windows and an old Camaro in my driveway, its rear end lifted up, its hood dulled with primer. After talking to David, I don't want to see Julián. I'd rather daydream.

"Hey," Julián says when I walk in. "Remember my friends from when we painted the wall?" They're sitting on the couch with their feet propped on the table and their shoulders slouched in boredom and fatigue. They've placed their drinks on my wood-burnings, watermarking my saints. I try wiping them off, but the stains are as stubborn as old scars, my portraits of St. Paul, St. Augustine, and Ruth ruined.

"How'd you get in here?" I say, irritated.

"The window. I didn't think you'd mind."

"He says you're his girlfriend," one of the boys says.

"Girlfriend?" It sounds like such a high-schoolish word. "You've been talking about me?" What did I expect after letting him kiss me and pretending to marry him at Bayfest?

"Well, you are my girlfriend, aren't you?" he says, his voice desperately insistent.

"Get over it," his friends laugh.

Julián gets a hurt look on his face, and I get protective the way I felt when I saw the beggar at the bank. I've put him up to this—offered a false hope that he's built himself up with. I don't like how these boys pounce on him with their bad-ass ridicule, making him the brunt of their jokes. Julián looks at his feet, and I realize that he has another life, exists in other settings where he's called names. But here he's Julián, his whole essence wrapped up in a slowly spoken name with long vowels, with "l" and "n," consonants my tongue can hold indefinitely, and to impose another name, to call him "pendejo" and "cabrón," to change his essence that way, is like drawing against the grain of wood.

"Sure, I'm his girlfriend," I say, shutting them up and enduring their up-down looks.

"And you're old enough to buy beer?" they ask.

"Of course I'm old enough."

"Well maybe you can get us some," they say.

"Well maybe you can get your feet off my table first." I slap their soles with a rolled up magazine.

"She's got a temper," one laughs, but they straighten up anyway.

I take my woodburnings to the kitchen, try to wipe them off again. Julián follows me.

"You mad about the pictures?" he asks. "Can't you do them over?"

"No," I say, holding them up, pointing at the grains so he can see the outlines of saints, but he doesn't. How do I explain it? It's not only my imagination that draws them, but my eyes and hands collaborating with the wood's rings. It's not possible for a saint's image to emerge from a different slab. I've tried it before, but the wood's lines lie against mine, making my drawings look like a child's indefinite scrawl. Julián picks up an image of the Virgin Mother, her hair a wild, windblown array about her face. He strokes the outline of her hair absentmindedly, follows the lines down her arm, stops and rests his forefinger on her open palm. I can see his deep apology, and I can't stay angry. It's like David said—it takes too much effort to stay mad.

"Go back to your friends," I say.

I heat some Pop-Tarts in the toaster. When I return to the living room, they're watching a late-night talk show about teenagers who've discovered their mothers were once pornography stars. They show film clips of these mothers engaged in trashy sex, Julián and his friends booing because of the thick black bands that cover everything but faces, feet, and dingy curtains and walls. "Put it on pay-per-view," one says. They laugh at the embarrassed children hiding their faces or yelling at their ex-porn moms. "Check it out, that kid's got a hard-on!"

They're ready to go when the show ends. We spend a few cat-and-mouse minutes at the door because Julián wants to kiss me in front of his friends, but I won't let him.

"Here," one of them says, handing me a Polaroid. "We took a picture of our last wall."

It's a photograph of an old hotel, its sign missing many letters, old tubs and plumbing where the walls have collapsed and exposed their privates like a woman with her blouse down. On the building's lower half is graffiti, not a mess of gang icons, but a picture, an old-time saloon with swinging-shutter-style doors, a woman sitting seductively on the bar, bare-legged except for garters and heels, and caballeros bluffing their way through a poker game. There's a large mirror reflecting the characters without flesh—the men with bullet holes in their skulls and yellow livers, the woman's womb with a skeletal fetus. It's a sketch more than a painting and lacks light, shadow, dimension, but I like the way it mirrors the building itself, which, like the people, is both alive and dead, both with and without its skin.

The boys get in their Camaro, rev its engine, alarming the dogs and causing curious neighbors to turn on the porch lights. When they back out, I hear my driveway's crunching shells. All the street's driveways are made this way except for those updated by cement, the homes of mollusks and crabs that once burrowed in wet sand now pulverized by the weight of cars. Once, a long time ago, I found an intact shell and kept it.

Julián and his friends finally speed off and things settle down again.

When I turn to go inside, I notice that the window shutters have been replaced. They've never been functional, just slats in a rectangular frame nailed outside my windows for decoration. Mr. Vela's patch-up job reminds me of the hamburger ads that hang in fast food restaurants, burgers too tall for any real person's mouth, an image that seems to ridicule what's really put in the bag, a grease-soaked sandwich with wilted lettuce and a paper-thin patty. Like the burger ads, Mr. Vela wants his house to project the American ideal—three bedrooms, a husband and a wife, two children, a well-trained dog named Fido. I've never seen families like this in real life—only in black-and-white sitcoms, children's books, or back-to-school flyers.

As I look at those fixed shutters, I realize that I've never had, in even the smallest degree, real ownership. My life here has been a myth that Mr. Vela has encouraged by knocking or waiting for permission before sitting down or accepting cups of tea like he was a guest and not the owner.

CHAPTER 6

The Statue

I t's still too hot for sweaters, even though it's late November. The trees are only beginning to lose their leaves. I know it's a natural process, but I can't see the beauty in the yellows, reds, and browns. It's as if I'm standing in one hot sneeze. The plants seem sick when they wilt, and I want to give them aspirin. I get the rake, cringe at the sound of its metal fingers against the cement, and am so focused on cleaning I don't notice Susie driving up. She laughs when she sees leaf crumbs in my hair and in the creases of my clothes.

"You're a sight," she says. When I look up at her, she seems like a sick tree, too skinny, her hair resting limply on her shoulders.

"They denied my loan," I say. "Something about me having bad credit history."

"Well, I always said no history's better than bad history."

Though it isn't Susie's fault, I want to blame her, anyway. "You're the one who talked me into getting that card."

She rolls her eyes. "But you've got to pay your bills, Sofía."

"I could have," I say, getting defensive. "It isn't like I was too broke to do it. I just forgot."

"How do you forget a thing like that?"

"I don't know. I get so many advertisements in the mail, and I can't always tell what's important. Or I put my statements in the

kitchen drawer and there they stay till I need some weird utensil."
What I don't share with Susie is my anxiety about losing this
house. I don't know where I'm going to go. I love this place, know
its quirks, and feel safe here. I don't want to live in an apartment,
to share walls.

She tries to cheer me up. "Well, Mr. Vela's not going to sell
right away," she says. "Didn't he say he'd wait till spring? You can
make a whole lot of money before then. Maybe we can talk him
into giving you a sort of payment plan."

"Like what? Rent?" I don't mean to be so sarcastic, but she's
not seeing the reality here. "The whole point of Mr. Vela selling the
house is to get a big sum of cash for his Winnebago."

Susie ignores my last comment, unfolds a copy of *The Corpus
Christi Caller Times,* and hands it to me. "Read this article,"
she says.

CRYING STATUE DRAWS HUNDREDS OF FAITHFUL

They stood in lines with rosaries, candles, Bibles, and binocu-
lars. They were the faithful, the reborn, the curious. Hundreds
flocked to Our Lady of Guadalupe Church on San Antonio's
West Side. In a line that snaked down several city blocks, they
waited to view a statue that appears to be weeping.

Above the article is a picture of a small church, everyone
shoulder to shoulder, staring up with both joy and fear, hope and
doubt. The Virgin Mary stands before them with outstretched
arms and open palms, her head sympathetically tilted. Draped
across her body is a cape whose folds curve softly. The people have
placed a simple, unadorned crown that sits off-balance, not quite
fitting as it should.

"I don't get it," I say because Susie doesn't believe in miracles.
"Read on," she insists.

There was also a long line of customers at the church's gift
shop for "artículos religiosos," such as candles of the Virgin
Mary that pilgrims lit and placed at the statue's base. By
Monday, this stand was overflowing with a multitude of candles
and bunches of flowers. Outside the church, a parishioner took
advantage of the opportunity and opened a booth where he sold
bags of potato chips, 12-ounce sodas, and dozens of tamales.

"Are you thinking what I'm thinking?" Susie says, her voice excited.

"I don't know what to think."

"It's a perfect place to sell things from our flea market booth. I can take all my Virgin Mary stuff. I just got a shipment of four dozen T-shirts, $14.99 apiece, but I'll let them go for twelve dollars if someone wants to buy two. And you can sell your woodburnings, start earning some money for this house. What do you think?"

"You want to drive all the way to San Antonio?"

"It's not that long of a drive. Just think of all the people who want to see this thing, all the money you can make." Her enthusiasm slowly begins to wash away my despondency over the rejected loan. She rubs her palms together, feeling the cash already. "For the house," she says. There's so much persuasion in her voice, and before I can change my mind, I'm inviting Chimuelita to come too.

"Yes, yes, come pick me up," she says. "I've got some things to ask her," and by "her" she means La Virgen.

We're at Pete's an hour later. We laugh as Chimuelita wriggles into her pantyhose and douses her hair with Aquanet before removing ancient pink rollers. She's already packed sodas into a small ice chest, which we load inside the Suburban already stuffed with the merchandise from our flea market booth.

"It's bad enough you have to take the day off," Pete says to me, "but convincing my wife to go too? What am I supposed to do? Run the restaurant by myself?"

"Come with us," Chimuelita pleads.

"To do what? Thank God for my freakish son?"

He disappears into his office to do paperwork, drink a beer, or watch the World Wrestling Federation as its competitors groan and grunt their way through the head butts and body slams of their choreographed bouts—anything to take his mind off César.

When we drive off, Chimuelita sits in the front seat with me, tries for twenty stubborn minutes to find her favorite radio station, the oldies-but-goodies. When she finally locates it, she joins Elvis by singing "Blue Suede Shoes" with a voice that isn't like Tía Lupe's at all but like that of a stray cat in heat, and we can't help laughing and mimicking those ridiculous noises of hers.

She's a good sport. "I lost my voice yelling at Pete all the time," she says before we lose the station and drift into that span of radio silence that lies between cities. Then Susie and Chimuelita talk about the upcoming wedding, and my attention drifts off.

Interstate 37 is straight, level, clean, and probably the easiest highway to drive along. There's a wide, grassy median between the lanes, an even distribution of rest stops and gas stations, and no wildlife except for the horses, cows, and occasional emu idling behind barbed-wire fences. The harvest is over, planting has yet to begin, and the land lies barren. All that's left are the crows foraging for worms in the upturned dirt and hawks circling the small farmland prey—mice, hens, rabbits, little dogs.

I was in San Antonio before when my mother volunteered to be a guinea pig for the Health Science Research Center, which was conducting a study on various allergy medicines. "With my luck, I'll probably get the placebo," she said, but she went anyway because she wanted the money for her time even though it barely covered the gas bill.

She needed to get a physical, and while I waited in the clinic's lobby, I watched the pope, who was visiting San Antonio. Every station showed his mass, but I couldn't hear what he said—only the flapping of souvenir T-shirts and flags and the shouts of vendors selling lithographs that pictured him waving one hand while the other held his scepter like a wand. After mass the cameras showed the pope riding through the city in a convertible car's glass box that made me think of collector dolls too fragile to play with or touch. A throng of people followed him like a dense flock of gulls trailing ferries. It was late afternoon by then. The sun's glare bounced off the glass of the pope's box, and for a second, the TV screen emanated a light so bright I had to squint against it. For minutes afterward, I saw only the light's green afterimage like a smeared moth on a windshield.

"You think we can watch the pope's parade?" I asked my mother as we left the clinic.

"What for?"

"It's a once-in-a-lifetime thing. It's not every day you get to see somebody famous." She ignored me and I became indignant beneath her apathy. "I saw him on TV," I persisted, still hoping to persuade her. "He's full of light. Pure light like . . ."

"Like what?" she asked. She gave a mocking chuckle, then a sideways glance that meant quit the bullshit.

She drove onto the freeway and right out of San Antonio, no comment. All I can remember is that life's mystery was drying up so fast, and I was only fourteen or fifteen or maybe even Julián's age. It's not that my mother didn't believe in saints, but she had twisted versions of their stories, repeating them as if they were fairy tales with the requisite "once upon a time," which made them even more unreal.

"Once upon a time, there was a nun named Lucia who had the most beautiful eyes in Sicily. When the king fell in love with her, she rejected him, and he had her eyes pulled out. The next thing you know, she shows up with a little twig, the blossoms made of eyes."

"But she could see from them, right?" I asked.

"No," my mother snapped. "And it serves her right. She could have lived in a castle if she wanted to."

For my mother, the saints were examples of how *not* to live since they were always being burned at the stake or losing their property or being regarded as lunatics by their neighbors. I tried to believe her, but when I started looking into wood, I saw the real story, and in the wood's version, Santa Lucia isn't a twig but a tall tree with dozens of eye blossoms allowing her to see beyond the horizon, beyond time, and from a hundred different points of view. She stayed true to herself. That's her real insight; that's what the wood—not the church and certainly not my mother—showed me.

Somewhere around the Three Rivers exit my mother's car turned off submissively, without first sputtering or lurching forward. We were out of gas. We coasted down a slight hill and my mother edged over to the shoulder where the car stopped in front of a big blue billboard—Gas, Food, Phone, One Mile.

"Well," she said, "now we walk."

She was calm in spite of being stuck on the highway with a teenaged daughter and only five dollars in her purse. She said a mile was only four laps around the track, that it was nothing, a stroll. As we walked, the highway boomed with sound—flies, leaves, birds, wheels on pavement. Occasionally something moved in the grass, or windmills, gates, and oil pumps squeaked. My mother jingled her keys and hummed Patsy Cline's "Crazy," and I began to wonder why we would stop at that exact spot, one measly mile from the station.

"Do you think," I asked, "that God knew we were going to run out of gas? That He's the reason we stopped only a mile away?"

"No," she said without giving it much thought. "Or we would have stopped in front of the gas station's pumps."

I don't know what I expected her to say. I felt the hot asphalt, blisters swelling on my feet, sweat stinging my eyes, and that pain in my side that comes from breathing out of rhythm. I started crying because I wanted the nearby gas station to be more than coincidence. I was growing tired of hoping for life's mysteries, but I was more tired of my mother's insistence on things as they really were. Couldn't she, for my sake, pretend?

She asked, irritated, "What's the matter now?" But how could I tell her? How could I explain that I had spent the day imagining a magical world because I needed it, because there, on the side of the road, where shreds of tires were strewn, where the carrion of skunks, raccoons, and possums lay split open, I needed to know that somewhere I had a father or a mother or a God who would not forget to fill the tank with gas?

When we get to San Antonio, the streets around the church are crowded. Most of the license plates are from Texas, but some are from Kansas, Oklahoma, Mexico, and other far-off places. The street is filled with more vendors than pilgrims. People are selling candles, flowers, postcards, tamales, second-hand clothes, used bikes. Susie can't find a spot for our stuff, so she pays a lady thirty dollars for letting us use her driveway. We set up, and as soon as we finish unpacking, Chimuelita grabs my arm and starts pulling me toward the church.

"You guys go ahead," Susie says, even though we've crossed the street already. "I'll take care of things here."

Chimuelita and I settle into a line leading to the church, and she begins to pray in a Spanish so rapid I hear only the atoms of words. *In the beginning was the Word—I give you my word, the word is on the tip of my tongue.* I break words up, syllable by syllable, until they are nothing but babble. When sounds are detached from meaning this way, all that exists is a voice's tone and there, I believe, lies the truth. It's why "love" is such a cheap thing to say—because it works in sentimental Hallmark cards as well as in seedy pick-up lines, because it refers not only to people, but to ice cream and favorite television shows. But Chimuelita's atomized words seem mystical, a possible avenue to the divine if I can keep from trying to interpret them.

"You hear that?" Chimuelita asks, grabbing my arm suddenly.

Someone starts to sing far off, a gospel song that travels down the line and becomes dense enough to drown out the vendors' shouts and the traffic noise. It follows us into the church where we stand between an old man in a brown leisure suit and a woman hiding beneath a long mantilla. I hear the communal voice undermined by the single strands of the old man's gravelly refrain and the lady's too-high soprano. The singing stops suddenly and there's only hushed prayer and money falling into the collection baskets.

I like this old-fashioned church with its incense, moldy marble frescoes, gold-framed portraits of Raphael's curly-haired angels, and stained-glass mosaics of Mary, Jesus, and Simon, their bodies crosshatched by gray mortar lines. The wooden pews have lost their luster and have been etched by nail files or pocketknives—Pablo, Sarah, Elena, Gail—and I think about writing my own address there, making it permanent with my pyroelectric pen. It's a beautiful little church but I get light-headed and weak-kneed when I genuflect because too many bodies are sucking up the breathable air.

"Do you see it?" Chimuelita asks, her voice a reverent whisper. "Do you?"

"Yes, right there." She points to the place where the tears should be.

I'm feeling dizzy. I look up and squint at the Virgin Mary's off-centered crown and welcoming arms, her carved and sanded smooth wood whose grain is lost beneath the paint. I didn't expect something miraculous, I admit, but neither did I expect such a dry inanimacy. I hoped for something slight and inconspicuous like a quick blink. I close my eyes for a long time, feeling more light-headed when I open them again, when I think I see a streak of moisture trickling down La Virgen's cheek.

"Chimuelita," I say, fainting before I can finish.

I hear Chimuelita's voice first, then an older Irish voice. I'm startled awake when someone waves strong smelling salts beneath my nose.

"Are you OK, child?" I open my eyes to a priest and Chimuelita glowing with pride beside him.

"Ay, m'ija, I'm so proud of you," she says, wiping my forehead with a damp cloth. "What did she say?"

"Who?" I ask.

"La Virgen."

"I don't know for sure."

"Then what did you see?"

"Nothing. I just passed out."

She seems disappointed. "You're a little confused," she says. "Give it time. That's how visions are."

I believe her because she's so confident, because she chose her husband based on a red feather and because a medicine woman cured her sister of fear. The priest says a Latin prayer and signs the cross on my forehead with his warm thumb. When we walk out, everyone moves aside and the old women touch my sleeves.

"Sofía fainted in church!" Chimuelita says when we reach Susie again, and the word travels around. Everyone comes to the driveway and instead of complaining about my saints, they marvel at them. I sell every single one. I give out our flea market booth's address in Corpus Christi so I can sell them there too. The people promise to come by. They promise. Even Susie runs out of T-shirts and candles. We've never been so successful and all because of a weeping statue.

When it gets dark and we return to the Suburban, Susie gets comfortable in the back seat again. "You know," she says, "I get such great ideas in the weirdest places."

"Like what?" I ask.

"Like the holy water at the store."

"From your kitchen sink? The bottles you sell for a dollar fifty?"

"Yes," she says. "I figured out a better way to market them. It's all in the packaging."

"The packaging?"

"Like when you buy perfume. Think about it. Who sells perfume in boring plastic bottles?" She waits for an answer. "Just go to Dillard's or Foley's. They use real glass. Sometimes it's tinted or maybe it's in a pretty shape, but the bottle itself is what gets your attention. After all, what's perfume but yellow water with a little scent?"

"Perfume is perfume is perfume," Chimuelita says.

"Exactly. What we do is invest in some attractive packaging, and then we up the price."

"Like selling holy water in an Obsession bottle," Chimuelita says.

"And charging an arm and a leg too." Susie laughs and so do Chimuelita and I. Most of the time I shut her out when she starts using her economic lingo, but what do I know? Didn't I just make a bundle of money thanks to Susie's idea?

I look at her through the rearview mirror. At the moment, I'm so grateful to Susie. I think she's smarter than me, but in the darkness, the mirror also reflects a tailgating car's headlights and my dashboard's red and green glow. A trick of light makes Susie seem transparent, turns her to a clear bag of skin, and I feel my faith in her slipping.

"Susie?" I ask.

"Yeah?"

And I don't know what to say next, so I mumble something about her being a good friend. I half expect Susie to laugh at me, but she doesn't. She says I'm a good friend too.

"And what am I?" Chimuelita interjects. "An old bucket in the seat of your car here?"

"No, no, you're our best friend," we say until she's satisfied.

Eventually Susie and Chimuelita fall asleep and things are quiet except for Chimuelita's snoring, which is both a deep guttural sound and a whistle merging with the wheels and the Suburban slicing through the air. It's dark without the streetlamps, and I enjoy not seeing the fence lines or the road's abandoned tractors. When we reach the Nueces River, the bridge's crossbeams wake them up and there's a sudden orange light and a sign: Entering Corpus Christi.

We reach the oil refineries—their white lamps glittering like gemstones, the smokestacks spouting fire, the tower tops like battlements, and the ocean behind like a giant moat.

"They look like castles," I say.

Susie holds her nose. "Those stinky things?"

In the morning, that mystical film over the world burns off, but the scene outside seems pleasantly disordered. The cars are parked along the road or on front lawns, a morning rain leaves puddles iridescent with oil, an old woman battles an overgrown hibiscus with her shears. I take my Maxwell House Coffee can, open its lid, and add yesterday's earnings, my loaves-and-fishes dream seeming true. At the bank, money is nothing more than a glowing digit on a computer screen or a dollar sign on a page of running ink, but here my money has weight, color, shape. It's stamped with the year of its birth and it speaks, "In God We Trust."

I notice that a crack in the living room has been repaired, the plaster like a thin, wavy tapeworm. This is the second time Mr. Vela's repaired something while I have been gone. I don't like the way he purposely avoids me. He's like a ghost—the fixed shutter, the plastered crack left here like Juan Diego's tilma—signs of Mr. Vela, but not Mr. Vela himself.

I go outside to get the paper, and when I turn around to face the house, I consider how it mutes the noise that keeps me from sleeping and opens its pores for cool breezes on hot nights. This house isn't a lifeless medium of exchange like Mr. Vela thinks. It's a living thing, organic, with enough sentience to know me, its resident for almost thirty years.

"You're alive," I whisper to it, and it responds by sloughing off a bit of paint and baring a palm-sized circle of wood. I start picking at the paint, which flakes off easily, and an image appears.

I run inside, plug my pyroelectric pen into an extension cord, and start to draw on the house's outside wall. First I hold the pen steadily and let the tip's weight do the burning, which gives the wood a smooth, even shading. I draw fine-point lines. Then I lean the tip on its side, letting it float on the wood's surface, which makes a fuzzy, indistinct line. I draw bold lines by pressing hard on the blade. I feel a deliberate gravity that seems to control the pen and the way I hold it. I'm completely lost in the wood's pale grain, which carries, in that paleness, an awesome mystery. I lose all sense of time, become deaf, blind, and irresponsible with the desire to finish this small circle of wall. In the end my drawing is too abstract to be a saint. Some might say it looks like nothing but a series of wavy lines, but if they look closely, they'll see that the lines move, independently—some slowly and others in quick bursts.

Susie's Store

On the morning news a shiny-toothed anchorwoman hides her aging neck beneath a bright red scarf, and her chimelike voice reports the auto wrecks, gunfights, and police car chases with their strobe light reds and blues flashing, surreal, on a tiny screen behind her head. The weatherman points to suns and clouds across the United States, football scores scroll down, a man writhes on a gurney, and I don't know what to focus on because everything seems equally important. Isn't there a war in the Middle East? Something beyond Corpus Christi? Something more pressing or more cheerful than the already wealthy man who bought a lottery ticket and won? Why him? He's got nothing to spend it on.

Susie's at the door. "Knock, knock."

"Who's there?" I say.

"Olive."

"Olive who?"

"Olive you," she laughs. I unlatch the screen, realizing that this is the closest Susie and I will get to the real words. Even on the drive home from San Antonio after seeing the statue and making lots of money, I shied away from admitting I love her. We grew up in the same neighborhood, went to the same schools, talk almost daily about clothes, movies, work, or Frank, but sometimes I want to talk when my brain's teeming with curiosities and ideas that keep me awake at night or in a reverie during the day. A few weeks ago, I saw a TV show about Percival Lowell, and what amazed me most was not his discovery of Pluto, but his psuedodiscovery of Martian canals. I couldn't keep from imagining his patient observations and painstaking record keeping night after long night.

"I didn't know Mars had canals," Susie said when I told her.

"It doesn't."

"Then what did he discover?"

"Nothing."

"So what's the big deal then?"

Sometimes I feel that we're having parallel conversations—speaking and even answering each other—but never connecting, not in any soul-mate way. We're like two trees whose branches are entangled because of how close our trunks are, our friendship a simple matter of proximity.

Susie props her foot on my table. "Like my new shoes? They're Cole Haans."

"They're what?" I ask, not knowing the brands of things.

She slips off her shoe, rubs her foot, sighs. "I like them, but they're killing me," she says. "Frank got them a size too small. He must think I have dainty feet."

She's wearing new slacks too, with a silk blouse and pearl earrings.

"Why are you all dressed up?" I ask.

"I'm a businesswoman now."

"What do you mean?"

"You'll see," she says, slipping her shoe back on. "I've got Frank's truck, but I need your Suburban too."

"For what?"

"You'll see. I told you."

I follow Susie outside and watch her disappear into the truck, her eyes barely above the steering wheel, making her seem like a child pedaling an oversized bike. I grab my keys without questioning her.

"Susie says instead of Simon says," my mother once told me. "If she asks you to jump off the Harbor Bridge, are you going to do that too?"

80

She was angry because Susie had convinced me to sneak into Mr. Silva's yard to steal his trash bags filled with beer and soda cans so we could sell them at the recycling plant. Susie wouldn't go herself because Mr. Silva posted Beware of Snake signs along his fence, but I wasn't afraid. He was my neighbor, and I'd seen him strategically placing plastic snakes around his yard, thinking they could spook a burglar better than a barking dog. I tiptoed into his yard, grabbed the bags, and tripped, the cans noisily spilling on the cement patio. Mr. Silva came bolting from his house with a broom.

"You little thief!" he shouted. "I trade those cans so I can buy me a doughnut and a cup of coffee in the morning. If I didn't have that to look forward to, I'd stay in bed all day!" He came at me as fast as his weak legs would allow, so I tried hurdling the hurricane fence, piercing my hand and ripping my jeans on the barbs.

I think my mother was angry because of my torn pants and the trip to the doctor, but not because I was trying to steal. After that incident, I'd feel sorry for Mr. Silva when I saw him hunting for cans in ditches, vacant lots, or in the dumpsters behind convenience stores, but that didn't stop me from following Susie around.

Today she leads me to the flea market, which is closed on weekdays, the empty parking lot like a pockmarked face, trashy after the busy weekend—wadded flyers, broken glass, discarded gum, crescent skid marks. Pigeons roost in the crevices of the Trade Center Flea Market sign, their nests a loose weave of weeds and candy wrappers. A janitor wipes smudges from the windows, and three heavy men sit at the curb.

"My hired help," Susie laughs.

The flea market's roof droops like a tired shoulder. The snack bar's stale garbage permeates the air. We walk past locked booths draped in white sheets or caged, only the memory of vendors shouting out slogans and children crying for cheap plastic toys and old women bartering for imitation gold. In the emptiness and silence, faces seem to peek from nooks and aisles—the Vietnamese family, the fat manicurist with tea-stained teeth, the man with the spiderweb tattoo—the building clinging to its imagery like an alcoholic to his beer.

I see stacked boxes and Susie's booth and a New Location sign with a map on hot pink paper. She unlocks and folds back the cage. "Let's get to work," she says without lifting a finger except to point and delegate. The three heavy men fold open boxes, tape the flaps, and load the baptism gowns, prayer books, chipped statues, and St. Jude magnets. They put the woodburnings left behind from our trip to San Antonio in a separate box and Susie labels it "Sofía's inventory."

"We're moving?" I ask.

"My dream come true," she says.

"Are you sure you're not overreacting to our success in San Antonio this weekend?"

"It's almost December, and I want to start the new year in a new place."

My Suburban seems to sink with each load. My wheels are sluggish with the weight, and I can hear a light glassware clatter as I roll over speed bumps or hit the brakes too hard. I follow Susie for a long time. She leads me to the suburban part of town, to acres of cleared trees and For Lease signs, to gated neighborhoods where the streets lack potholes, graffiti, and poor valley farmers selling sandías and lemons from their trucks. The neighborhood names refer not to Corpus Christi's flat coastland, but to hilly pastures and log cabins by peaceful ponds—Meadow Park or Swan Valley—idyllic promises of a rural life's simplicity with water clean enough to lap from streams and grass without burrs or anthills or shards of glass. We finally pull into a shopping center, Deer Springs, a smooth, hot lake of pavement and bushes clipped to look like pyramids or scoops of ice cream.

"You're moving here?" I ask, noticing the scents of fresh paint and recent carpet shampoo when I enter a little store.

"Why not?"

"It's too far out."

"For us, maybe, but not for the customers."

"What customers? Our flea market customers aren't from around here."

"Exactly," she says. "That's why we couldn't move the big stuff. We've got spenders out here. Just look at their houses."

What Susie doesn't understand is that she sells not merchandise, but hope. People buy her candles because they believe the flames contain the spirits of saints. I've seen them spinning the turnwheel where we keep the prayer cards, searching for words that fit their lives, words for the sick child, the dying parent, the endless bills. We cater to the needs of the desperate. Why pray when the car starts faithfully, when it doesn't rattle along the highway? Why pray when the house is air-conditioned, the appliances quietly work, and the roof keeps the rain out? Why pray when even the dog is dipped once a month and kept clean enough to sleep at the foot of the bed?

"Who's going to buy your stuff here?" I ask.

"Everyone needs God, Sofía. Not Prozac but Prayer is my new motto." She laughs and jots it down in a little notebook.

So we unload. Susie has the layout in her mind already and knows where to place the boxes that must wait for the tables and shelves to arrive. She points to track lights illuminating the back wall, tells me I can hang my woodburnings there, that they'll sell because the people here are more sensitive to art.

The three men sweat and strain without complaint, an electrician adds a ceiling fan, a Southwestern Bell man installs a telephone while we flip idly through bridal magazines.

"Which dress do you like best?" she asks, sliding a magazine toward me.

She's already marked the pages with Post-its. What strikes me are the models, the way their skin lacks hair, bumps, or wrinkles, their premarital glows nothing more than tricks of lighting. Is that what Susie wants? That type of paper doll face? She applies her makeup meticulously, and if she were tall and full-breasted, she might look like them. Her taste in gowns leans toward the sexy side, bare-shouldered and low-cut with flared skirts and long trains. After twenty pages the gowns become indistinguishable to me. Susie wants my opinion, so I riffle through the pages and my finger lands on eighty-two.

"What about this one?" I say. She looks as if she's never seen it before.

She's placed Post-its in other books too—a china catalog, a travel guide, a book of wedding cakes—everything extravagant.

"The wedding is only a one-night deal," I say, trying to imagine Susie and Frank handling life's daily drudgery—spitting toothpaste in the sink, washing day-old dishes, spraying Raid on large, flying roaches.

"My one-night deal," she says as she gives the workers a bundle of bills and writes checks for the telephone man and the electrician.

"Where did you get the money for this?" I ask when the workers leave.

"Frank."

"Frank? And where did he get the money from?"

"His savings."

"You're taking his savings?" I ask, mad at what seems like an injustice. Here she is spending money like it's as abundant as air while Frank's working his ass off and I'm scanning floors for dropped pennies.

She gets defensive. "I'm not taking his money. It's an investment. Why the guilt trip?"

"I'm just trying to look out for you," I explain.

"You look out for me?" She seems genuinely surprised. "You're going to complain about me borrowing a little money from my fiancé when you've spent your whole life borrowing from others?"

"What do you mean by that?" I ask. "I don't borrow." She gives me a yeah-right look.

"Frank's going back to school," she explains. "At night. To be a doctor like I said."

I'm feeling mean—childish-mean—the kind that pulls hair, throws things, chants *so so suck your toe*. I'm stuck on Susie saying I live off others. Who's she to talk? I'm more independent than she'll ever be.

"Frank doesn't want to be a doctor," I say. "He's happy sticking thermometers up people's butts and feeding drooling men. You're fooling yourself thinking he's going back to school."

The minute I see her hurt eyes, I regret what I said. Maybe our friendship is based on more than proximity. If I were to measure it in terms of time, it would seem invaluable. I've got to cling to the good things Susie does like letting me hang my woodburnings in her store and never cheating me out of money. Isn't that, in this day and age, the best friendship a person can have?

"I'm sorry," I say, really meaning it. "I just think you should hold off for a while."

Susie's already beyond forgiveness. "Hold off? For what?" she asks. "Let me tell you about my father because there was a man that liked to 'hold off.' All he ever did was spend money on gambling, the jackpot always at the tip of his fingers, according to him. 'Almost won.' That's what he'd say when he came home. And he isn't a mean man, just irresponsible. He likes to have his fun, try his hand at the gambling wheel before paying the bills, but I get mad because my mother works the skin off her hands for us. I ask her why she stays with him, tell her we'd be better off alone, but she just calls his gambling a 'disease,' says he can't control it. When she does complain, my father acts embarrassed, like a child caught doing something bad. She forgives him, and instead of buying herself a new pair of shoes or pretty clothes or getting her hair fixed, she gives him more money. Well, I'm out of there, Sofía. Frank and this store are my ticket out."

I want to tell Susie that this store's a gamble just like her father's bets and card games, but I can't find a break in her conversation.

"Remember that house my mother cleaned on Ocean Drive?" she asks and I nod. "One day I went with her so we could go to the movies afterwards. It was my birthday or maybe I made good grades. She asked the lady if she could leave early, and the lady didn't seem to mind. So my mom cleaned the kitchen, the floors, the pee around the toilet. When we finished, we went to the lady, who was sitting on the couch with a big glass of tea and a magazine. My mother had her purse and had already put lotion on her hands. She told the lady we were through for the day, but the lady pointed to a wall of windows and said, 'You haven't cleaned the blinds yet.' My mother didn't even argue. She just got the bucket and the rag again, and after she started to clean, the lady said, 'Each blade. The undersides too,' without even looking up from her magazine."

"She was just being mean," I say.

"She made me feel small. She meant to keep my mother from ever asking to leave early again." Susie closes her magazine and stuffs it forcefully in a book bag. "So don't make me feel bad about opening a store, Sofía. I'm never going to wipe up another person's pee or clean where no one ever looks. And I'm never going to waste my money on chance."

The phone rings, Susie answers it, and after a few moments her voice gets light again. I know it's Frank by her girlish laugh, her finger coyly curling the cord, her body's flirtatious stance. She turns away from me and speaks softly.

Sometimes I can't bear to hear Susie complain about her father. At least she knows him well enough to say he's foolish with money. I grew up thinking I just appeared one day, a basket on the doorstep like a biblical child, always insisting that my birth was something unexplainable even after learning biology. My mother would get angry when I asked about my father. "It's not a fairy tale," she'd say. "You'll end up feeling disappointed." I just wanted a picture, something clearer than the black-and-white photograph she claimed was her only image of him. It's a picture taken at the beach, my mother sitting on the hood of a '56 Chevy in a bathing suit and pointy-rimmed sunglasses. I see how thin she is and how her bikini top promises a glimpse of breasts that aren't really there. My father is holding the camera, the sun behind him casting his shadow across the car. All I can say with certainty is that he wore a fedora. At least Susie's father is more than a shadow or a name on a birth certificate yellowing in a rusty cabinet somewhere.

"What did you do to my house?" Mr. Vela says when I answer the phone. He's never yelled at me like this before.

"What are you talking about?"

"You vandalized it, burned it with that pen of yours!"

"I didn't just burn it. I drew a picture."

"Of what?"

"You can't tell?" I'm not going to explain it. He probably drove by the house and glanced at the wall without stopping to really examine it.

"How am I supposed to get rid of those lines?" he says. "Who's going to buy the house with a scar like that?"

"It's barely larger than a page, and besides, I'm going to buy the house. Don't worry about it."

"You got the loan?"

"No, but I plan to make enough money for it. It's not for sale yet, right? You said I had till spring."

"But you violated your lease," he says quoting something about needing approval for certain things.

"What lease? I never signed anything."

"Your mother signed it. I still have it here. You're responsible for the cost of any damages." He lectures me about the terms of this mysterious lease, and I can't believe he's kept it all these years, after calling me "m'ija," after inviting me to his house for holiday barbecues, after saying "I need to fix your sink, your light, your ceiling fan" as if I truly owned these things. I imagine this lease in his clutched hands and I realize that I live here not because he wants me to, but because I submit my rental check on time. There are rules to follow, and breaking them could get me kicked out.

"Here I am trying to make things decent over there, and without any respect for me, you mess the place up!" This isn't the Mr. Vela I grew up with, his scolding voice making me feel like a child with a dunce cap. "I'm getting too old, Sofía, to worry about things like this."

"Well, don't worry. It's taken care of," I say, hanging up before he can respond.

Things aren't much better at Pete's. I walk into the restaurant, and instead of greeting me, asking how my day went, or offering me a plate of food, Pete glares like a bull waiting to charge.

"Where were you yesterday?" he says, his voice barely containing his anger.

First Susie, then Mr. Vela, now Pete. I'm not in the mood for anyone else's bitching. "Well, I wasn't at work," I say.

He clenches his brows against my sarcasm. "We tried calling you, but you didn't answer the phone."

"I was too busy to answer it."

"Too busy?" He breathes in deeply with nostrils that could swallow a hand. "If I didn't have a business to run, I'd have gone to your house and dragged your ass over here myself."

"Dragged my ass? What are you being so huffy about? This isn't the first time I took a day off."

"You took two days in a row," he says. "I had to close down Monday when you took Chimuelita with you."

"Well, you're the one who busted up Parker's face and threw César out."

I know it's an unspoken rule not to mention César's name. Pete flinches when he hears it. But he's being hostile now and like a cornered boxer, my only recourse is to hit him where he's soft.

"He'll come back," Pete says.

"Is that what you think? Because it's been two months now. Why don't you hire someone else to take his place? It's no wonder I took the day off. I'm tired, Pete. My feet ache, my wrists feel weak from holding the pitchers and trays. If César meant to come back, he'd be here already."

"He'll come back," Pete says, louder. "He's just trying to spite me, but he'll come around. You'll see."

"You're fucking dreaming, Pete. He might as well be dead to you."

When he gets that hurt expression, Chimuelita suddenly plows through the kitchen doors, a rolling pin in her masa-webbed hands. "Ya, Sofía," she says, "¡cállate!"

"You're taking his side now?"

She waves that rolling pin in my face. "We took you in when you were an orphan girl, and God knows I love you like a daughter, but that doesn't give you the right to talk ugly to my Pete." Then she says, with a sternness I've never heard before, "It's about time you start earning your money and your free meals." She points to a bucket of soapy water and I feel like an exploited Cinderella sloshing away.

CHAPTER 8

Percival Lowell and the Martian Canals

Julián raps on the door and gets a suspicious look when he sees me in my black spaghetti-strap dress and too-high heels. I've got plans with David, who asked if I'd like to go to a reception at a bank where he painted another mural. Pete says David's a regular fixture the way he's been visiting the restaurant these past few months. He sits and grades papers if I'm too busy to talk. Sometimes he helps me clean up when the restaurant's ready to close so I can leave earlier, but he hasn't invited me anywhere before now, not even down the street for hot chocolate. The bank reception we're going to is a Valentine's Day affair. This time I didn't give him the let's-be-friends line because I don't want to screw up again or wait another ten years. I'd like to see David in another setting, but what I really hope for is that speechless communication I see between Chimuelita and Pete, César and Parker, and even Julián and his friends.

I see a spot of blood on Julián's chin. "What happened to you?" I ask.

"I shaved," he says, and the way he proudly rubs his jaw makes me laugh. "What's so funny?" he asks self-consciously.

"Nothing."

He stands at the threshold and gives me another suspicious look. "What are you all dressed up for?"

"Nothing," I say, even though I've spent the last thirty minutes before a mirror applying makeup and pulling my hair into a French braid so tight it almost slants my eyes. It's a weak attempt at sophistication.

"You going out on a date? Because I thought you were my girl-friend."

"No," I lie again. I tell him I'm going to dinner with Susie and Frank. "I'd ask you to come but it's a dress-up thing," I add, guessing that he doesn't like suits and ties.

"For Frank's work?"

"Yeah, for Frank's work. A lot of boring doctor and nurse types are going to be there."

He accepts it, though he seems disappointed. The way he so readily believes me makes me feel guilty. But why am I lying anyway? He's just a skinny kid that likes to come by. Cute, but a kid nonetheless. I should end things with him, but I can't explain it, can't give him that I'm-too-old-to-be-your-girlfriend line again. He's living this little fantasy, and I don't want to be the one who screws it up. Let him meet a sweet girl at school. Let him forget about me that way. I kiss his cheek, meaning to say good-bye, but he grabs my waist and kisses me back, sloppy on the mouth, his face like a messy clown's with my lipstick.

"You need to go now," I say, urging him out the door till he mounts his bike and disappears around the corner.

Thirty minutes later, David arrives looking uncomfortable in his tie. He squints the way he does when he's embarrassed, and we stay on the porch a few moments before I tell him to wait inside while I lock the back door. When I return, he's looking at my scattered wood-burnings—St. Peter, St. Teresa, St. Anne—which seem to squirm beneath his scrutiny. He stops at the Seven Sleepers of Ephesus, who are returning to their cave after seeing a modern city with its smokestacks and traffic-cluttered roads. They'll sleep another two centuries and maybe they'll wake to a different world or no world at all. He doesn't say anything, but he has an understanding smile.

I wish my mother understood—not necessarily what I drew but my desire to draw. When I told her I wanted to study art at Del

Mar, she laughed and said it was a preposterous idea, throwing out the syllables like bad food, her tiny spit-drops on my face.

She came to an open house at my high school where Ms. Sullivan, my humanities teacher, displayed one of my sketches, Mary Magdalene sitting on a pedestal, her ankles crossed, her blouse at her waist, her long hair over the cusps of her breasts, dark love bites on her neck and upper arms. It was one picture amidst a whole wall of art. One student drew demonic gargoyles, another painted wildcats with dismembered arms in their jaws, a long-haired boy stood before it all and recited phallic fruit poetry, but my mother took offense at *my* work.

She said, "I'm not sending you to school to idolize prostitutes."

The next day she got Ms. Sullivan in trouble, complaining to the principal that she'd let me draw nasty pictures and withdrawing me from the class because she didn't want me following a "fool's dream." What made her such a pessimist? She could never look at me, her own daughter, and go beyond motherly duty to that thin tightrope of trust and risky love. I was her project, her blank wood, and instead of letting me follow my own dreams, she tried pressing her own upon me.

"You should be a nurse, Sofía, or a teacher. Drawing's what you do in grade school, not something you can make a living from. That's why they say 'starving artist.' Think about it. Have you ever heard of a wealthy artist? Or even a middle-income one?"

She was practical like Pete. For her, art was as foolish as César's wanting to fish or needing Parker. I know it's bad to think this, but sometimes I'm glad she died when she did, before she took that one last dream I clung to. My school counselor got me all kinds of money since I was an orphan, and I went to school for three years before I ran out of classes to take. I couldn't move on to the university without the core curriculum, but I didn't care. I figured I knew enough.

I say to David, "You're the only one who really looks at my work."

"You're the only one who really criticizes mine."

At the bank there's valet parking and a red carpet that leads to the lobby's entrance, but David's driving a faded Honda Civic, towels

91

on the seats to keep the cracked vinyl from snagging our clothes, buckets of tempera paint, chalk, and a roll of butcher paper beneath the hatchback. The thought of his car beside Volvos and Cadillacs makes us laugh, so we park down the block and walk to the bank, the February wind fiercely trying to unbraid my hair. This bank's no different from where I applied for a loan—marble floors again, glass walls, indoor ficus and palms, a chandelier whose lights aren't as brilliant as those at the oil refineries.

"I want to show you my mural," he says, leading me to a narrow, curved wall where he has painted Selena again, this time like Botticelli's nude goddess standing on a giant shell, except that David's floats above Corpus Christi's gulf, her loose hair flowing over her hips, breasts, and a long line of thigh, with floating zephyrs replaced by reverently bowed fans. It's colorful but one-dimensional, the evenly blue ocean lacking waves, the too-round sun, the grainless sand without grass or sandpiper footprints. Selena stares, expressionless, medieval. I would have given her haughty eyes. I would have made the fans jealous, greedy, or sexually aroused.

"How creative," some women behind us say.

"It reminds me of the painting behind the makeup counter at Dillard's, don't you think?"

"Yes, the one with the angels in the sky and the blond woman standing on a shell."

"You mean Botticelli's *Venus?*" I ask.

They twist up their brows. "Bottle who?"

We find a corner of the lobby set up like a living room—sofas, end tables, lamps, weak with a soft 40-watt glow. We sit on a loveseat, uncomfortably quiet because we're in a setting to talk. The lobby's forced nature—the horseshoe arrangements of furniture, the dimmed lights, the melting Cupid ice sculpture, the women cradling single-stem roses, and everyone coupled off— makes me realize I'm participating in some elaborate love game and I'm surprised by how readily I dress the part even though I'll never be anything but a waitress, a fact imbedded in my posture, a certain perpetual stooping over for leftover dollars and change. The bank's people glide by like specters, their voices nothing but a static din.

A string quartet sits in a circle of light, three tuxedoed men and a woman, their faces half-hidden behind music on thin metal stands. The woman's knees constrain a cello, which seems no dearer to her than her chair. She has a white, angular face like those Victorian-style figurines in the back corner of the flea market's trinket booth. She seems to fight her body's natural suppleness, stiffening her legs, locking her elbow, her bow strokes jerky. Wide-eyed, she concentrates on her fingers' rigid march across the cello's neck. Maybe she has no instinct for music, her Bach and Vivaldi without a rhythm for my toes to thump the beat to.

"Come here," David says, taking my hand and standing up suddenly. "There's this woman I want you to meet."

He takes me to a crowd centered on a woman in a white dress that scoops below the waistline of her purposely malnourished back, her skin dark and wrinkled from too many hours in the tanning salon.

David politely waits for a break in the conversation. "This is Sofía," he says to her, "the friend I was telling you about."

She gives me an up-down look, regards me as if I were a garment for sale. "I have a room," she says, "a sun room." I give her a confused look. "I'd like you to stencil an ivy on my wall," she explains. "Nothing too difficult. You wouldn't need to draw anything. Just copy. Neatly. And add some shadowing to make the leaves look real."

I'm already shaking my head. I thought David understood my art when he saw the woodburnings earlier, but here he is trying to turn me into a craftsman.

A waiter offers us hors d'oeuvres from a silver tray—little bite-sized appetizers I don't know the names of. When my cracker crumbles to the floor, the waiter shakes his head as if I were a clumsy child and snaps his fingers twice, alerting a maid who sweeps the mess into a dustpan, then returns to her dark, heavily draped corner. Everyone else's cracker survives.

David says, "I thought you might like the job since you're trying to get money for your house."

I turn to him and see nothing but rescue in his eyes, a fairy tale running through his brain. I appreciate his intention, but he's crazy if he thinks that stenciling this lady's wall will buy me a house. She'll give me a handful of change after a hard day of work, and it'll add up to nothing but a few pizzas and maybe a tankful of gasoline.

"I only draw saints," I say to David pointedly.

"Yes, dear," the lady tells me, "but I've a sun room, not a church."

I excuse myself, say I have to go to the bathroom, and when I look back, I see David shaking her hand the way he shook Pete's when he agreed to paint his wall. When I realize how readily he accepts these odd jobs, how he's going to paint her wall because I won't, I feel tired of the whole fucking world. I don't know how I fool myself into thinking he's got the will to be true to himself. For enough money, he'll paint anything.

I wait in the restroom's line while watching a woman purse her lips at the mirror and rub her feet before putting them back into their cramped Valentino heels. In the stalls there are tissues to line the toilets, sterling waste disposals with Kotex icons, and polite Please Discard signs. The stark contrast disgusts me; the thought that outside consumptive beggars plea for change while I could live my whole life in this restroom and never catch a cold.

When I leave, David's waiting outside the door. "Why don't you just think about it?" he asks.

"You want me to sell out?"

"It's not selling out. It's being practical. I thought you had a house to buy."

"I do. I've got a whole coffee can of money I'm saving."

"A coffee can?" He half laughs at this. "You're never going to get anything, Sofía, if you don't give in to how the world works." I stand there with my arms crossed trying to think of a comeback. "This isn't even my scene," he says. "I wanted to get you a job." He stands there for a few minutes and takes off his tie. Then he looks at me like I'm something delicious. "You ever been to Doc Rockets?"

Doc Rockets is a blues club. We walk into its thick, smoky fog, the people silhouetted against flickering candles, their cigarette tips glowing red. We find a small table, order a pitcher of beer and a bucket of messy buffalo wings, and listen to the crowd's murmur—blurred, diffuse, and weightless as if speaking underwater—a wavy language with a rhythm I unconsciously sway to.

"You never told me what you thought about my painting," David says.

"Because you didn't really paint anything," I tease. "You just took two images and pasted them together. Where's the art in that?"

"Where's the art?" he asks defensively. "It's in the arrangement of imagery. It's no different from what you do with your saints."

"It's completely different."

"How so? You take old images too."

"But I don't paste them together. I wouldn't take a picture of Jesus and make him Elvis. I just follow what's already in the wood."

"You're telling me there's no intention in your work?"

"I don't impose imagery, if that's what you mean."

"So if you had a completely clean surface, no lines, you'd leave it blank?"

"Sure. What's there to discover? Isn't that the purpose of art?"

"No," he gently counters me. "It's to create. A blank surface is like all potential. You can put whatever you want there, even a creature no one's ever seen before."

"Now you're contradicting yourself."

"How?"

"Because you haven't created anything yet. Just a few moments ago you told me art was arrangement. Where's the creation in a Selena that looks like La Virgen or Botticelli's *Venus*? You're better off painting Selena as herself."

"That wouldn't be art," he says, "but portraiture."

"When Michelangelo sculpted his *David*, he didn't really create as much as free an image from the marble. You aren't freeing anything when you draw. You're just locking things up."

He pauses a moment. "Sometimes you're ruthlessly honest, Sofía. Couldn't you just tell me what I want to hear?"

"What's that?" I ask.

He doesn't answer. I watch him thinking and putting all kinds of words in my mouth. When he takes another swig of beer, a drop trickles down his chin and across his outstretched neck before disappearing behind his shirt's loose collar. Then, because he took me from that listless bank and brought me to this looser place, because I think he'll understand, I ask him if he knows who Percival Lowell is.

"No. Who is he?"

"A scientist," I say, "who thought he saw canals on Mars. He even mapped them out."

"There aren't canals on Mars."

"I know, but he was convinced. I realize it's silly, but he's like a hero to me."

"That's not silly," David says. "You admire him because he was a scientist who should have based his conclusions on facts, but instead, he let his imagination interfere. He stood against the evidence staring him in the face, and still dared to believe."

When he hits the point exactly, I suddenly want to share all my far-fetched ideas, but before I can say another word, the bar gets quiet as a black, voluminous woman fills the spotlight's circle on the stage. She wears a red satin dress that supports her insurmountable breasts with boning and a band like a weightlifting belt around her torso. Her name is G, a cursive letter on a placard surrounded by elaborate curlicues, the bare essential of a name that could stand for Georgia, Geraldine, or even a treble clef G as in "Every *good* boy does fine." She's got a voice like sangria—thick, earthy, with intoxicating undertones.

> I've got some bad habits
> Lord, help me please.
> I've got some bad habits
> Lord, help me please.
> I leave the house walking
> But crawl back on my knees.

After a few songs, she says, "Let's scat!" The pianist plays a riff and then G completely discards coherent language and becomes a vocal trumpet, sax, and drum—her lyrics a string of furious phonemes. I discover sound's concreteness, that no word is as sinister as a hiss, as soothing as a hum, as lively as a tickity-tac-tac. I want to be G, to swim in her voice.

David and I get on the dance floor and stand so close I don't know where his body begins.

"You're not going to kiss me tonight?" he asks, following me inside my house and putting his tongue in my mouth before I can answer. He walks me backwards toward the couch where he hooks his foot behind my knee, buckling it and making us fall, keeping his mouth pressed so hard I can feel the razor stubble above his upper lip, his weight gently suffocating me till he props it on one elbow, his mouth finally granting me air while his teeth lightly run along my clavicle and nudge my dress strap from my shoulder. I can taste the faint residue of beer and smell the bar smoke still lingering in his hair. He stops a moment, rests, breathes like he's just climbed stairs, toys with my dress's scooped neckline, lowering it one slow inch at a time till it falls beneath my breast. He looks at me in a way that makes me quiver, and he kisses me again, this time with a softer urgency.

I just think we're kissing, making out the way teenagers do, till I feel his hand running along my hips, till I realize how high above my knees my skirt's hitched up, till I feel him hard beneath his zipper's cold metallic teeth against my thigh.

I wriggle away from him, stand up, return my strap to its shoulder.

"You're going to leave me hot and bothered?" he asks, playfully approaching me.

I back off. "This isn't some coy game."

"Then what is it?" he asks, getting serious.

"I just want you to go home—now."

I realize that my voice is cracking, that I sound a little scared, and maybe that's why he doesn't leave. He just stands there confused. And what do I say? I can't tell him that the thought of sex makes me remember my mother's open door and all the faces that pounded her while she listlessly looked at the ceiling fan.

"Will you go home now?" I urge.

"No," he says. "What's the matter? You still a virgin?"

He's speaking gently, calmly, but I feel so exposed. I can't stand the way he tries to figure me out like I'm some puzzle to solve. Who does he think I am, anyway? Some nineteenth-century holdover?

"I'm supposed to fuck every man that walks through that door?" I say.

"Is that what you think? You think I'm here to fuck you?"

"It makes sense."

"I'm not a monster, Sofía. I just want you. I want you in every way I can think of."

He sounds hurt, but I'm too flustered to stop myself. "Well at least Julián doesn't come in here and push me down the way you do," I charge.

"Julián?" he says, getting angry. "That teenager from Bayfest? You let him in here?"

"He practically has a key."

He shakes his head. "What's the matter with you? You shouldn't be hanging around kids like that." He starts toward the door.

"It's easy to leave now, isn't it?" I say, pleased and hurt at the same time.

He turns around. "You come find me when you're ready for a real man," he says, and then the bastard slams the door.

I stand in the darkness while his Honda's engine fades off. Then there's only the fatal buzz of moths as the porch light singes their wings.

9

Neither Out Far
Nor In Deep

I n Corpus Christi spring slides in. There isn't that seasonal shift marked by a leafy outburst, only a gradual warming, a deepening heat and humidity. It's an early Saturday morning. I knock at the restaurant, and a tank-topped Pete scratches his belly and throws me a confused look before unlocking the door.

He asks, "What are you doing here? It's Saturday."

"It's Susie's wedding day. Chimuelita's going to help me get dressed."

"What do you need help for?" he teases. "You're a grown woman already."

"Let her in," Chimuelita calls, and when she tells him that we've got some girl things to take care of, he cringes with disgust and waves me upstairs where Chimuelita waits, sipping coffee as she sits on a tattered recliner, her feet up and ready to be polished.

"What does Pete think 'girl things' means?" I ask.

She giggles. "When we were young, things were a lot different—not like now when men are willing to film their babies being born. When I was pregnant, Pete walked a big circle around me, wouldn't even come in the room if I was breastfeeding or changing the baby's diaper, wouldn't even burp them like it was so gross, like he never burped himself." She laughs so hard her breasts almost avalanche free from her robe. "We're one big mystery to Pete," she says, clenching her toes and cracking them. Then she gets a bit serious. "Are you ready for this wedding? Did you invite your friend David? Maybe you can give him some ideas."

"No," I say with a don't-ask-about-it voice. "I haven't seen him in several weeks."

"Weeks? I wondered why he wasn't coming anymore. You got in a fight already? What's the matter with you, Sofía? Don't you feel sexy about him?"

"What makes you think it's my fault?" After she gives me that I-know-you look, I try changing the subject by offering to polish her nails. The last thing I need is a birds-and-bees talk, but there's no stopping Chimuelita once she's started.

"Just show him your body," she suggests. "You'll soften his heart and harden the rest of him. It's like the song says, "Love makes the world go 'round." I get quivers just thinking about it."

"Well, David's too pissed off to give me any quivers," I say.

"So it *is* your fault. I knew it. You've got to quit living in limbo, Sofía. It's the worst place to be. Take Pete. He hates and loves César but he's too wimpy to do anything either way. You and Pete have to make a decision, stick to it, and pray that things work out."

"Maybe I can paint your toes now."

"Because you can't make things happen by yourself. Like my uncle who went to the San Juan mission in McAllen. He made a promesa—no haircuts for five years if God cured him of cancer. It wasn't like now. Back then, it was really bad for men to have long hair."

"Was he cured?"

"Of course."

"Just like that?"

"No, it took a while. He had to go through the chemo first."

"Then maybe it wasn't God," I say. "Maybe it was the chemo."

"It wasn't the chemo!" She almost swats me with her hair-brush. "I'm telling you it was God. My uncle got fired from his job because he had long hair. Do you think he'd do that if he thought for one minute that chemo saved him?"

Maybe she's right. Lots of people go through chemotherapy and die anyway. Maybe her uncle's barter with God did save his life, but what has God done for me? I prayed rosaries for my house, I fainted in a church, but that didn't stop my loan from being denied or convince Mr. Vela to stop the sale.

We get to work on our "girl things." I trim and file Chimuelita's toenails because she's too fat to bend over and do it herself. She's got old, plump feet, with gorged veins, bristly toe beards, and calluses from walking in chanclas. Her nails are an opalescent yellow, and when she squeezes into her pumps, her foot fat bulges out the sides. She wears fake lashes, a Marilyn Monroe mole on her cheek, and a hairdo teased up into a sixties beehive. We have to safety-pin the spaces between her dress's buttons because they can barely contain her huge boobs, but it's better than my dress, whose sleeves puff out like the floaters kids wear when swimming. Pete takes ten minutes to get dressed. He stays in his work clothes, a white grease-dappled shirt and navy pants, but he adds a tie and trims his sideburns for the occasion.

Before we go, I wrap Susie's present, a woodburning depicting the wedding at Cana where the newlywed couple ladle money from stone jars into the guests' cupped hands since Jesus has changed the water not to wine as his mother requested, but to gold coins.

At the church, a nun directs a few reluctant teenagers who mumble "peace is flowing like a river," and whose bored guitarist sits too close to the microphone, strumming a dull down-up-down-up rhythm, his fingers scratching their way along steel strings. He's got black nails, eyeliner, and hoops on his brow and nose like a heavy metal guitarist. Maybe he's here to please his mother or to fulfill some Sunday school requirement. The nun claps three times and there's a revived interest in the song.

While Pete and Chimuelita find a place to sit, I wait for Susie in the vestibule where an old lady drops her coins into a slotted metal box and lights a candle. She winces as she kneels to pray; the fires before her are small, contained, with insignificant wisps of smoke and flames I can snuff out with my fingers' moist pinch. I see the woman's eyeballs roving behind her lids and her veins pulsing beneath her tightly clasped hands. She stops uttering her Spanish petitions and I help her stand up. Her knees leave shallow depressions on the cushions, but they disappear as soon as the foam fills up with air again. I think about Chimuelita's uncle, drop all my change into the slotted box, kneel, and force myself to believe that a few extra coins might get me more money or convince Mr. Vela to change his mind, and what I say exactly is I'd like a home. I wait for an answer but all I hear is Susie calling. When I turn to face her, she's waving to me, her fingers wet with holy water.

In the church dressing room, Susie's mother, aunts, and brides-maids tuck, pin, and button her dress, the aunts' arthritic hands and the bridesmaids' long, acrylic nails barely managing the tiny buttons that run down Susie's back and sleeves. She stands on a platform like a mannequin, the bridesmaids hovering. She picks up her skirt and reveals her skinny, pantyhosed thigh. "Something blue," she says, laughing and pointing to a blue satin garter. I don't want to hear the something-borrowed-something-new part, but she recites it anyway, pointing her foot, which I squeeze into a sequined shoe that reflects the light like glass. She gives us combs with dull plastic beads and crimped tulle, which sit in our hair like white weeds.

Susie's wedding is like every wedding I've attended—a white dress, a unity candle, a lazo, rice, and las aras, but this church isn't like the church in San Antonio. It has no incense, no frescoes on the ceiling, no wishes etched into the pews. The only artwork here is a stained-glass window, and when the sun shines through it, the reddened light of a Roman's tunic settles on Susie's veil.

A woman at the podium stutters an Old Testament reading, her eyes avoiding the congregation, her voice pausing at every fidget, cough, or sigh. She's probably worried about her blouse's buttons and whether or not there's cleavage, about the way her neck's sudden change of tint marks the boundary between her liquid foundation and skin. My missalette rustles as I frantically search for the words my mother kept me from memorizing. I say *thanks be to God and praise to you, Lord Jesus Christ* a beat too late, my voice wearily trying to converge with the crowd's but rubbing against theirs and against the choir's lazy "Amen." Everyone else sits, stands, and kneels simultaneously but I am one second out of sync.

When Father John says *repeat after me*, I hear Susie's rushed *in health . . . for richer . . . till death do us part*, against Frank's

102

loud syllables savored like the sweetest fruit, his silver tooth shining as brightly as his wedding band. When we stand in line for communion, I hear the mumbled *body and blood of Christ* and the whispered *amens*. The wine goblet's rim is cool and dry because it's wiped off after every sip, and the Eucharist rests between my palate and tongue, a cool penny until I swallow hard.

After mass, an organist labors over the music like a child just learning to read, and I follow Susie and Frank out of the church where we shake the guests' hands. Then Susie grabs me, her rings biting my fingers. She says, "See you at the dance," but I've decided not to go because I can't smile my way through this anymore. This whole ceremony feels like an elaborate act. It isn't sincere. I won't dance to "Europa" with the sweating best man or take Susie's money for the dollar dance as she twirls on the floor with drunkards that will hold her tiny waist with their hooflike hands. I can already imagine how she'll tilt her head back and laugh. *I'm not stopping till I've danced with every man,* she'll say. *Twice!*

A rain of confetti falls as Susie and Frank stoop into a limousine decorated with streamers, a Just Married sign, and strings of cans. The parking lot empties out. Chimuelita and Pete say they're cruising down Ocean Drive before the reception.

"Do you want to come along?" they ask.

"No."

They don't press me. I wait until the last guest leaves. The priest stands in his hot robe, rubbing the sweat from his brow, and then he walks into a liquid blur that rises from the asphalt followed by the altar boys, the tallest one with a too-short robe that shows his faded jeans beneath. He walks with a stumbling pace, as if his legs haven't adjusted to his sudden height—graceless like me. Tucked under his arm is the processional cross, and on his feet is an oversized pair of hightop shoes branded with a meaningless black squiggle. I heard those shoes are worth a lot of money, that a kid in Chicago was murdered for them.

I'm out of my dress and into a T-shirt with blue jean shorts five minutes after walking through my front door. I'm about to nap when I hear Julián calling through the screen.

"You want to go to the carnival?" he asks, glancing back at his friends kicking rocks across the street.

"Are they going too?" I ask. Julián doesn't answer, but one of the boys is already taking a box from the Camaro and putting it in the back of my Suburban. The carnival comes every April for Buccaneer Days. I'm not sure I want to be tossed and twirled in some rickety machine, but it's better than going to Susie's dance or waiting for the phone to ring.

Buccaneer Days celebrates pirates, even though no one's proved that any actually came here. I once read that Sir Frances Drake landed along the Gulf coast for drinking water, not predicting the Spanish would destroy all but two of his ships, which couldn't carry both Drake's men and treasure home. Rather than lose their plunder, more than a hundred sailors volunteered to escape on foot, or maybe they drew lots or were simply pushed overboard. That's all I know about pirates near Corpus Christi, but even if Drake's men did nothing but pass through, we celebrate Buccaneer Days the way we celebrate Christmas, Easter, and the Fourth of July. We wear eye patches, striped cutoff shorts, and pirate hats with crossbones and skulls, and push the mayor into the sea. There's a carnival, fireworks, and a parade with high school bands showing off, with floats sponsored by Miller Lite, Coca-Cola, and the YMCA, and things get lax everywhere—beer vendors forgetting to check IDs, security guards ignoring the minor brawls, cars parking along the red tow-away zones.

On Suicide Day, the day after the rides' rushed assemblies, the carnival is free till 7:00 P.M., as long as we sign a waiver to keep us from suing for injuries in case a few bolts fall loose. We get on the Super Loop, a rattling yellow caterpillar that hurls us up and around a big metal circle. Julián yells, "Whoa!" like he's on a too-fast horse. We ride the Zipper, the Himalaya, the Sizzler, the Monster, and a big Viking ship that rocks until it flips us upside down. Julián and his friends choose the most daring seats, ride without holding on, and run like eager pups to the lines. At the Fun House we laugh at our stretched and twisted reflections in the mirrored maze. Then the Wagon Wheel spins us in too many directions, makes the clouds and ground a psychedelic blur, our screams both delighted and afraid as we test how much stirring our stomachs and brains can take. I like to give up caution this way. Gears and pistons are more predictable, more trustworthy than the way David squints sometimes or Susie's wedding or Chimuelita's reliance on prayer. We walk off weak-kneed and nauseated and one of Julián's friends—the fat one—vomits over an exit-ramp rail. Everybody laughs, even the children walking by.

"Shut up," he says, offended. "It's those fucking tacos I ate for lunch."

"You wimp . . ."

"You should stick to the carousel, cabrón . . ."

"Or the little train . . ."

He spits and runs a comb through his hair. "That train can't move with a fat fuck like me," he says, making the boys laugh till their eyes tear.

We find a booth where Señor Surprise is doing an elevator card routine, making the jack of hearts magically rise to the deck's top after being placed at the bottom or middle, the boys begging to know how it's done. "I don't reveal my secrets," Señor says, but when they slap down a five, he tells them about the double lift. "It's really two cards. See?" He spreads them out. "You think there's only one, no? But when I put them on the deck, I slide the one on top, not the jack like you think. I put it in the middle, wave my hand, and 'poof!'—but nothing really happens. It just looks like the jack moved, but no, it's always there. ¿Comprende?" He demonstrates a few more times, but even though we know the sleight, we never see that extra card.

"I always thought it was real magic," Julián laughs despite his disappointment.

"Don't be stupid," his friends say. "Even when they chop up those girls, it's only some fake legs you see."

We've been on all the rides. The boys decide to waste some money in the arcade tent, but I wait on a bench outside listening to the arcade's gunshots and laser blasts, its men shouting "step right up!," its quarters cascading from the change machine.

Then I glimpse a young contortionist across the busy street, a waif in a white-hooded bodysuit with socks and gloves, her brows pale against her sunburned face. She stands on her hands, her back toward me, and slowly bends back her legs, deeper, deeper, till her feet stand flat. That's odd enough, but then she tilts up her head till her body's a perfect backward O. Her smile flickers through the crowd's brisk legs like light through branches. I study her face, hoping for some brief communion, but she unrolls herself and curtsies at the applause. She seems to defy our sense of reality by bending into the most unnatural shapes, by curling her bones. She does the seemingly impossible and people drop coins and dollar bills into a nearly full hat.

Inside the arcade tent, I find Julián at a combat game.

"Who are you?" I ask.

"That blond guy," he says, keeping his concentration. His blond counterpart is a Viking warrior with abnormally large abs and pecs, with a loincloth and boots laced to his knees. He defeats over and over again some primordial beast, green and twice his size, with claws and spits of lightning which the warrior throws back with a mirrored shield. Blood spurts everywhere as the combatants grunt. I watch Julián's reflection on the screen, colors flashing across his face—the bright lightning bursts, the reds and oranges of the beast's blood. Julián bites his lower lip, relaxing only during the interlude between battles as he waits for the beast to reincarnate itself. He smiles back at my reflection, and in one bright burst, the Viking warrior is scorched by the beast. YOU HAVE NO MORE LIVES flashes across the screen and wisps of smoke rise from the warrior's charred bones.

"I think we're ready to go now," he says, waving to his friends, who've packed my Suburban with bonfire wood, a boom box, a shoe box of tapes, and an ice chest of beer.

On our way to the beach, we drive along Ocean Drive, and I don't think I'm asking for much when I compare my little home to the large bayfront houses. We cut through the Seaside Cemetery where Selena lies. Even now a crowd gathers at her gravesite and leaves letters, pinwheels, Selena-style dolls, photographs, and flowers in cans wrapped with colored aluminum foil. The men kneel and the women bow their scarved heads as they utter prayers they think she will answer. Nearby, children stir up anthills with sticks, gulls pick at leftover food, and stray dogs dig into the fresh dirt at a burial site.

106

At the beach we turn right at Bob Hall Pier, drive beyond the Kleberg County line till we find a lonely stretch of sand near an old-fashioned outhouse with a moon carved in its door. We get out. Unload. The boys take the wood and make a log teepee for the fire.

I leave them alone for awhile, go to the shore and stare at the jellyfish, a turtle rising for air, the crosslike wingspan of gliding gulls, and a pink-and-blue sunset with two clouds, thin as fingers, sliding slowly apart like a father reluctantly releasing his child's hand. I suddenly want to find my mother's sandbar and stand on the water the way she did. I take off my shoes and step into the ocean, which is always warm, even in winter when it steams as if exhaling hot breath. Half-immersed, I anchor my heels against the currents, the lowest tide urging me deeper, the uppermost waves shoving toward the shore, and the middle currents swaying left and right. My feet are invisible in the water's murky brown, but I try to see through it, anyway, curious to know what lurks between sandbars.

If I lift myself and float the way my mother did, I can ignore the water's push and shove and contend only with the surface and its one thin layer of resistance.

I swim and relish the peace till a speedboat breaks the silence, its curdling water catching a swell and turning over in a fast-approaching wave. I try to withstand it by pointing my toes to the ground, but I can only tread water because I'm too deep already. The wave hurls its weight on me, topples me, and presses me down until my cheek hits the rippled floor, my whole body immersed in this place reserved for whales, eels, and flounders. But I don't panic because the force holding me seems gentle. I imagine my mother still swimming in this nether land between sandbars, or God hiding his secrets from us without gills or exoskeletons to keep us from imploding beneath the sea's great weight. I open my eyes to the stinging salt, to a shape—a fin, a shell, an oil clod—one tangible truth in this amorphous place. I try grasping it, thinking it can be known and understood, but it eludes me. Then I'm spit out. When the water washes away, I'm only knee-deep, and the jellyfish aren't jellyfish at all but plastic grocery bags, and the turtle a green bottleneck.

107

"That's all?" I ask the sea, whose only response is a weak slapping.

"You went under," Julián says, anxious and out of breath from running toward me. "All I saw was your hair."

"I'm okay. It was only for a second."

"What did you see down there?"

"Nothing."

"No fish?"

"No fish at all."

The water falls in a thin sheet over him and reflects the sun's pinking light. I expect to see a greater density in his body—a muscle swelling above his knee or biceps, a manly thickening—like David—but Julián's still thin, stumbling backwards every time a wave hits.

We find his friends beside the splintered gray outhouse. One shakes a can of black paint and sprays a vertical line that widens and grows fuzzy in the porous wood. The second boy makes a tree of the line, and Julián draws a guppy, half-turned away, with a tail like a fringed shawl, thick-lashed doe eyes, and scales like silver coins. They stand back and nod at this guppy that floats in air and breathes oxygen with such ease. Then they paint their spades on the bottom corner.

"You like?" they ask me.

"Very much," I say.

Julián lights the bonfire, which fills the air with a mesquite aroma and dries off my hair and clothes. It's a beautiful fire, especially against the dunes and setting sun, especially for me because I have only known the fires of candles and gas stoves—fires I can extinguish with a dial or a forceful breath, unlike this one whose flames lash out, ripple the air, and beat like a loose screen door. In its yellows and reds, the figures of saints softly emerge—St. Joan of Arc and St. Polycarp—and then they disappear. The boys throw in mollusk shells that pop in the cinders.

Then we make a smaller fire, set up a grill, and boil water in my stew pot. We all run to the shore to catch the crabs clumsily scuttling across the water's edge, their claws like toothed pliers. There's a contest to see who can catch the most without getting pinched. I don't know who wins—not me or Julián, who puts a nicked thumb to my lips so I can kiss it and make it better. After our hunt we drop the live crabs in the stew pot and their claws scrape the sides frantically till there's nothing but the bubbles' hushed explosions. We take them out with tongs after they've boiled and set them on paper towels to cool. Soon the night beasts venture out—mosquitoes and dune rabbits wary of coyotes howling not at the moon, but at our flames.

The boys take out their boom box and put in a rap tape of urgent words. We drink beer and pass around a joint, its scent weak against the burning wood and sea. I put it to my mouth, the paper still moist from their lips, and I inhale, trapping the smoke to let it simmer and seep into the tiniest of pores, till my bones and brains are smoke-soaked. The music on the boom box is beating like pistons and I move with it even though the lyrics are too fast and the tempo too much like a speeded-up monk's chant, foreign and numbing, but devout. Soon there's nothing but the particles of words—syllables, accents, silent *E*'s.

We pass the crabs around, peel off their undersides to get at the meat, white and flaky, discarding shells that lie about us like dirty dishes strewn on the floor. The tape clicks to a stop, but no one plays another.

One of the boys takes a pair of pliers from his pocket and a wire hanger, which he puts in the fire till it's red-hot. He shapes the soft metal, makes a lopsided spade, removes his shirt, his back nothing but taut skin and faint shoulder blades. He tells me to burn his back with the hanger. I see his stoned eyes and hear his speech like a slow motion movie. I remember Susie's wedding ceremony, how well arranged it was, how the white dress symbolized the chastity of a Susie who is not a virgin, how the rings symbolized a union that will not last if Frank fails to become a doctor. But here things seem natural. A fire and four boys who hope to seal their brotherhood not with words, but with a sign.

"Bite on this," I say, giving him a small towel and heating the hanger till it glows red. In one firm stamp I singe his back. He tenses up but makes no sound against the burn that will blister, swell, and dry into a spade-shaped welt.

"Bite on the rag," I say to the next boy.

"Okay."

"Bite on the rag," I say.

"Okay."

Then Julián offers his back, and I get the notion I can make a man out of him so I press the hanger hard and unrelentingly till he lets out a painful cry and jolts away.

"What the hell did you do that for?" he says, the crescent moon above his head like the emerging horns of a prepubescent ram. The other boys laugh. "Shut the fuck up!" he says, throwing fistfuls of sand at them. Then he says he's got to use the can, and he disappears behind the outhouse while we pick at oil clods stuck to our feet. When he comes back, he's got tear-swollen eyes and an accusing expression.

"You told me to burn your back," I say.

"I know," he answers, grabbing my ass and giving me an abusive kiss, which leaves little tooth hyphens on my lips. I push him away, but he just laughs and starts loading the Suburban.

On the way home, the boys lean forward to keep their burned backs from the seats, and when I see a sign advertising itself—342-Sign—I realize that I've broken my own rule, that I've burned an image where it doesn't belong.

"It fucking hurts," one of the boys says, and I have to pull onto the road's shoulder, lean out, vomit, and convince myself that I'm sick from smoking, beer, and boiled crabs.

Cat's Nite Club

Susie thinks that the secret to success is a matter of finding the right jingle, the right sign.

"Remember Wendy's with their 'where's-the-beef' campaign?" she says, leaning on her store counter and drawing a line that goes nowhere on a hot-pink poster.

Business is unbearably slow. Susie passes her time by inventing useless tasks like dusting and rearranging the shelves, wiping windows, and making signs with her poster boards and markers, but for me, time is stretched out futilely like a baby's arm reaching for a mobile that hangs too high above the crib.

"Maybe you should go back to the flea market," I suggest.

"Never."

"But . . ."

"But what?"

"You were making more money there," I say, regretful when I see her downcast eyes. I glance at the wall where my woodburnings hang and see my version of St. Anthony of Padua, the saint of lost things. He's standing on a heap at a public landfill where angels sort through debris and gulls hover above mounds, his face hidden behind a newspaper's large page, its headline—YOU SEE?—the question mark looming large. I don't want Susie's dream to end up on that heap of lost things, but there aren't any customers in this overstuffed shop. She's got cards, candles, books, music, statues, jewelry, even gardening things, but all she's sold today is a baptismal bib.

"Things don't happen overnight," she says optimistically. "You have to see them through. Kids will be making their first communions in May and then everyone will get married in June." She clings to this false hope. Sometimes I wonder if she'd listen to me if I were an accountant, an insurance agent, or the man who restocks the soda machine—someone with an education or a decent credit history.

Susie plays church music on the stereo—Gregorian chants, chorals, nature tapes of waves and gulls—music that lacks the energetic beat of Tía Lupe's strumming, Julián's rap, or G's scatting at Doc Rockets. Susie's music moves like slow sludge, lulls my thoughts and makes them turbid. I could probably fall to sleep standing up.

Like Pete, she keeps her place cold and beads of condensation run down the windows where we keep a mannequin dressed as a nun, her lips pursed for sweet whispers or kisses and her figure too seductive for someone who's vowed celibacy. Susie found her in a dumpster behind a department store. It's missing a leg and some kids spray-painted a penis on its torso, but none of that's evident beneath the heavy robe which hides everything except her pert nipples. A passing lady glances at the mannequin and quizzically raises her brow, but she's more interested in the soda machine outside. When she digs in her purse for change, she doesn't find any, so she opens Susie's door, makes our little cowbell jingle, and closes her eyes when relieved by the air conditioner.

"Can I help you?" Susie says, her voice regaining that familiar lightness.

The lady shrugs. "Just looking."

I see Susie's hope drop like a stone in water. She knows that "just looking" means the lady has nothing in mind, that she's cooling off while she wonders what store to visit next or what to cook for dinner. I never knew how many bored people there were till I came to this part of town. The customers at Pete's always stop by on their way to someplace else because his restaurant is

112

cheap and convenient and because they don't have time to simmer their own beans or roll their own tortillas, and the flea market's customers are lively, darting in and out of booths, loudly bargaining and laughing because they don't shop as much as spend time with their families. I'd watch grandmothers pushing strollers, teenage cousins eyeing boys, and children playing hide-and-seek. But the customers at Susie's new store walk in listless and alone. I've seen ladies enter while their husbands are at work and their children are at school. They dress up because they have closets full of clothes and nowhere to go, because they believe that life's like a soap opera, that a two-hour outing warrants linen skirts and gold jewelry, and when they accidentally run into each other, they share little cheek kisses that are quickly wiped off with delicate pats of Kleenex and speak formally as if quoting some prim etiquette book.

The lady finds a bookmark with St. Francis speaking to attentive birds, *for it is in giving that we receive.* I remember my woodburning, how Chimuelita nailed it to her living room wall. This lady will probably put St. Francis in a Harlequin Romance book, which will yellow and end up on a Goodwill shelf. I scan the UPC code and a zero-point-twenty-five glows blue on the register's screen. She rummages through her purse again.

"You'd think I'd at least have a quarter," she says, pretending to be surprised. There's her Mary Kay compact, a comb, a cellular phone, and a billfold of credit cards—Foley's, Dillard's, Visa, Exxon. She sighs while giving me a twenty. "Would you believe?" she says. "This is the smallest bill I have, and this bookmark is an absolute must." I give her the change, and as soon as she's outside, she buys a Diet Coke from the machine.

"Well . . ." Susie says, her voice dropping off.

I might have let the incident go if Susie hadn't realized that the sale was just a cheap means to a soda. I know I complain about how lightly she takes things, but I don't like her dark, gloomy side either. Maybe it's better to live with flighty dreams than to accept a reality that isn't working out.

Impulsively, I run out of the store. "Hey, lady," I say. "Why play this stupid game? You think I didn't see you looking for change before you came inside?"

She looks at me like I'm some ax-murderer. "You stay back," she says, "or I'll call my husband." She reaches in her purse for the cellular phone, dropping her Coke in the process.

"Why don't you just tell us you need the change?" I say, following her menacingly and making her toddle in her dainty high-heeled shoes.

"I've got mace here," she stutters. "You better leave me alone or I'm calling the police."

"And what law am I breaking? You're the one who fucking lied! Who's playing games with my friend!"

I don't feel guilty when I see the way that lady fumbles with her car keys and jumps inside too hurriedly to notice her skirt sticking out the door, the way she screeches out of the parking lot with her ear to the phone and sissy tears running down her face. I think justice is served. I think I'm doing Susie a favor by getting rid of that bitch, but instead, she's pissed off when I return.

"You're fired!" she yells, half crying.

"What?"

"That lady's husband is going to walk in here and I'll have to apologize and brown-nose my way out of this mess!"

"You don't have to do anything," I say. "We don't need their business."

I've never seen her so mad. She acts like she doesn't hear me. "It'll be a whole lot easier," she says, "if I can tell them I fired you. Maybe they won't give me such a hard time."

"That lady lied to you, Susie. She made you feel bad."

She gives me the angriest look I've ever seen. Her upper lip twitters and she blinks wildly to stave off tears. "Well it's nothing compared to how bad I felt last week when I got married," she says.

"When you got married?" I don't make the connection. "What are you talking about?"

"I'm talking about you not going to my dance. What kind of person disappears from her best friend's wedding? Everyone was asking, 'Where's Sofía, where's the maid of honor?'"

"I didn't think I'd be missed at the dance. I thought my part was over after mass."

"You're supposed to be my best friend. You aren't supposed to pull disappearing acts like that. Even Pete and Chimuelita were wondering where you were."

"They never said anything."

"No one ever says anything. You live in a damn box, Sofía. You want the whole world to fit into it—even that lady. She pissed you off, not me. You're yelling because of your own principles. You're mad because she wanted change to buy a Coke while I'm just glad to get twenty-five cents from her."

Who's really in a box? I want to ask. That lady only pretended to be interested in the store, and Susie's crazy for thinking twenty-five cents is worth feeling grateful. I feel like clapping my hands in her face to wake her from whatever dream she's in, but she's glaring at me and telling me to leave.

"Susie," I say tentatively, "you can't fire me. You need me here."

"For what?" she says. "What service do you provide? I'm paying you what little I have, trying to get you money for your house, and all you do is complain about the way I do things." She points her long fingernail at the door. "Get out of here before that lady comes back with her husband."

I don't have anywhere to go. I drive toward my neighborhood, cruise down Ayers and flinch when I pass the corner where my mother died. I still have a whole afternoon before work. I've never seen Susie this angry before. Usually I'm the one clenching my teeth while Susie's laughing.

I wander aimlessly till I find myself parking across from Travis Elementary where David works. I think being near him might make me feel better. His school is a windowless, cylindrical building that almost looks like a detention center. I like old school buildings better because they have breezeways, windows, and little courtyards between the wings. A bell rings and a few minutes later, children stampede out the doors and into the playground. Some teachers follow, David among them, and they post themselves at opposite corners of the field to watch the children play dodgeball or dizzy themselves on the merry-go-round.

115

I wish I hadn't thrown him out that night. I could talk to him right now if he weren't mad. I've convinced myself that his interest was an illusion. I won't let myself believe in happily-ever-afters, but at the same time, I won't accept anything less. When I think of getting close to him, my mother's voice reverberates in my head—warning me, daring me.

I see David lean against a tree, and I want to honk my horn to get his attention. I want to tell my mother that she's full of bullshit about men—that she was full of bullshit the day we drove down Ayers. I was absentmindedly looking out the window at a theater that once had an old-fashioned façade with an ornate marquee and a shell-like niche with a lion's head and water spouting from its mouth into a pool. I used to make my wishes at this pool, throw pennies over my shoulder, hear them plop, and close my eyes while waiting for them to come true. I'm still waiting, I guess, but the lion's gone now and so are the coins. Inside, the theater's seats were velvet and the walls were painted with murals of blossoms, peacocks, and vines. The screen had two gold brocade curtains with fringed hems. One would rise, the other would open sideways, and this subtle sweep of fabric was enough to hush us, to draw our heads forward. I was so eager to give my dollars to the smiling teenager in the ticket booth so I could lose myself in a movie—*Godzilla*, *Tron*, or a Walt Disney cartoon. Before it closed, Ayers Theater was perfect, but on the day my mother died, it had a sign advertising not movies, but a church, one of these new churches, the kind that don't have histories.

That was what I was thinking about moments before I noticed our car fast approaching a red light at the corner of Baldwin and Ayers. I tried telling my mom to stop, but she didn't hear me because she was transfixed by the bright pink wall of Cat's Nite Club where a silhouette of two dancers waltzed, the man in a tuxedo, the woman in a fifties-style ballroom skirt. Cat's Nite Club isn't even a ballroom. It's a seedy bar. Through its open doors, I can still hear men shouting obscenities, fighting over pool tables, and catcalling as they try to pinch the waitresses' asses. Today the bar wall flaunts a rabid wildcat, but back then it captured a moment of perfect grace.

116

My mother ran the light, a truck slammed into us, and our car flung itself against a pole.

When I woke up, paramedics were already trying to reach us. I looked at my mother and saw an awful fusion of body and machine, but she was awake and talking.

"Your father came from an island far away, and for his birthday, his parents gave him a huge silver kite that he liked to fly by the ocean. The children would watch and hold its string, a string that was three blocks long."

She was repeating a storybook I once had. "What the hell are you talking about?" I said, more scared than angry.

"Then a storm suddenly appeared with winds strong enough to lift your father and the children. They saw their houses getting small below them. They heard their parents crying. They held on for a long time, but they were above water and getting tired. When the winds died down, they drifted to an island."

"You're delirious, Mother. They'll get us out soon."

"The children wanted to go home, but the kite couldn't lift them without the winds. It could lift your father, though, and he went in search of their island. But he got lost and landed on Emerald Beach where we met." She was ad-libbing the last part. The island boy never landed near Corpus Christi.

When she saw my confused face, she let out a wry chuckle. "You're the one who wanted a story," she said.

What was I supposed to do? Did she really expect me to imagine a blue-watered beach, women in soft wrap-arounds, and men so proud of their chests they walked without shirts? Was I supposed to accept that my father was some selfless man leaving me for a higher good?

"This is our moment of truth," I whimpered, "and all you can give me is some fairy-tale crap?"

My mother closed her eyes and laughed the most horrifying laugh I had ever heard. I couldn't tell if she was mocking me for entertaining hope or praising my skepticism. She fainted and a blood bubble expanded at her mouth's corner as she breathed out. I thought it might dislodge from her lips and float off like a balloon, but it burst instead and red-speckled her face. She died three days later, but she never spoke again.

I don't want to be like her, to give into a fantasy, to risk being used, to become apathetically promiscuous the way she was, but ever since David put his tongue in my mouth, I can't shake the taste of him.

A child throws a ball past his tree, and when he turns to fetch it, he sees me. I think he's going to smile but he just stands there staring, not at me exactly, but through me the way I sometimes stare through people or things. I feel paper-thin. I try to smile, but he turns around, throws the ball to the children, and returns to the tree, keeping his back to me.

Will you fucking turn around? I say under my breath, and if this weren't an elementary school, I'd march up to him and throw a book or pour paint down his shirt—something, anything, to make him acknowledge me.

When the bell rings again, he and the other teachers round up the students and return to the building. He's so tall next to them. The children jump beside him, trying to reach his shoulders and hanging from his arms and legs, and he bears their weight with a playful patience. When a little girl stumbles down, he kneels beside her, stands her up, brushes the dirt from her knees, and holds her chin in his hands to calm her crying while another child, a rambunctious boy, jumps on him for a piggy-back ride to the classroom. Now that I see him at work, I realize that he never meant to be an artist. Teaching's his vocation. He didn't just settle into it like I had thought. He really loves these kids. He's been true to himself the whole time.

I'm home for five minutes when I hear, for the first time, the doorbell's gentle chime. When did that get fixed? It hasn't worked in years. It was probably a loose wire that took Mr. Vela fifteen minutes to replace.

"Why don't you just use the key?" I say when I see him at the door. "You don't hesitate when I'm not around."

I feel like being a bitch to the whole world. I've got nothing but threadbare hope now. Susie and David won't look at me, I burned a scar on Julián's back, and Mr. Vela keeps hinting that he's almost ready to start selling the house, though he tries to hide it by looking like he always has—jeans, a cowboy hat, an anchor with Jesus hanging from his neck, and a concerned expression that's hard to believe since he's been no more than a pesky ghost haunting my place, not by breaking but by fixing things. I once anticipated his visits. I baked apricot cakes if I knew he was coming—my mother's recipe, though she stirred the batter with an unprovoked vengeance. Maybe it was my father's favorite cake. Maybe she baked it the day he didn't show up. I look at Mr. Vela's chapped mouth and consider offering a glass of tea or juice, but I resent the way he let me believe I'd always live here, that this was my house. The way I see it, he both planted and uprooted me. And what's he uprooting me for? A Winnebago? Well, I hope he has a good time.

"Why are you here?" I ask.

"I want to let you know that I'll be doing some major repairs now."

"What's left to fix?" I ask because he's done everything already—shaved the tops of doors that wouldn't close right, replaced the bathroom's mildewed boards, balanced the wobbly ceiling fans, and planted grass. He stopped trying to be sneaky about it.

"I've got to take care of the outside now, get those burns off."

"You're going to get rid of my woodburning?"

"It brings down the value of the house."

"Brings down the value? It's not even that big."

"Well, this place really needs a paint job."

I can't convince him that my woodburning gives this house character. If I stare long enough, the lines undulate and quiver against the wall like guitar strings. What else do I have here? What's mine besides memories so fragile they crumble beneath time?

"Look," Mr. Vela says, "I'm too old to do the work myself, so some men will be here Saturday. I'll tell them not to bother you."

Saturday morning, a team of men in white coveralls unloads gallons of paint, rotary sanders, brushes, ladders, and an air-compression machine that will make a quick job of whitening the walls. Layer by layer, they peel off the old paint and sand away my woodburning, their scratching and scraping making my house seem like a flea-bitten dog. I hide in the hallway, the only room without windows, without their shadows crawling over me. After they've sanded, there's nothing but the tender, chafed skin of wood, its grain's thin lines branching out like spider veins. I swear the house shivers at the slightest breeze. Then I hear the air compressor's harsh whir as it spits out pellets of paint. When they finish, the painters peel the tape from the windows, and the house flinches like a child when the Band-Aids are pulled. Then they drive off.

I stare at my rusty Maxwell House can, which seems like the stump of a rotting tree. Everything's slipping away. People and places. And money too.

La Curandera

Maybe I shouldn't have talked so meanly to Mr. Vela and the lady at Susie's store. I wore my throat out with so much bitching, lost my voice to an infection intensified by the humidity and the steam of plants growing and overgrowing—mesquites, crepe myrtles, oleanders, and weeds proliferating in sidewalk cracks or in the small patches of dirt that collect along the street's unused curbs. I can smell everything, the allergens like severe irritations in my nose. When I swallow, two tight fists grip my neck and my breath barely wrenches itself between them. I lie on the bed, my movement nothing but a rolling back and forth like a door on its hinges.

When I call Chimuelita, my voice sounds raw. "I think I'm too sick to come to work today," I say because I don't want Pete yelling at me again.

"You got any eggs?" she asks.

"No."

"Well, don't worry. I'll be there in a minute."

She's ringing the new doorbell soon after we hang up, a carton of eggs in her hands and a floppy beach bag with her medical supplies. Her face droops with concern, and her "pobrecitas" make me wonder how terrible I look. She puts a cool, damp cloth on my forehead, checks my pulse, and takes my temperature, uttering knowingly under her breath. The room seems to tilt when she sits down, her weight making a huge valley at my bed's edge, and even when she stands up again, she leaves a deep, warm depression beside me.

"I called my friend," she says. "She'll fix you right up." But I'm asleep before I can answer.

When I wake up again, Chimuelita's friend is moving about the room, her bones grating loudly. She must be a hundred years old. Brown bags of skin on her upper arms sway loosely, and her dress against her belly and breasts hangs in curious folds that form elusive shapes. Her face's wrinkles are shallow, but the skin below her chin sinks to her chest. She's got cataract-blue eyes, lips curled over the potholes of her gums, and white hairs that spout from her scalp like forceful geysers.

She closes the curtains to darken the room and, with meager muscles, moves the bed and me to the center where the ceiling fan hangs directly above me, its pull chain bobbing. I don't want to believe in this curandera crap. If magic were really possible, then I'd have enough money for the house. When I try protesting, nothing comes out, and I keep slipping in and out of sleep. When she lights a stick of incense, it doesn't glow, but gives off only the remnants of fire—smoke and ashes sifting down. When she speaks, there's only her mouth slightly parting and her wild, whiplike tongue. I don't understand her, but I think she's asking me if I renounce the devil and all his wicked ways.

If I could, I'd tell her to quit the bullshit, but I'm too weak to resist.

I think I see Chimuelita in the corner with a frying pan and a bowl from which the woman takes two eggs, icebox-cold, putting them in my palms, and folding my fingers over them. She takes another egg, and when she rubs it over my soles, I imagine my fever rushing into it and its sizzle as she cracks it into Chimuelita's pan. She rubs my whole body with eggs, pressing them close to the point of breaking, so that I feel, though they look perfectly smooth, their monstrous pits and knobs. She manages to cool parts of me that feel unbearably hot—the area under my chin and the crooks of my elbows and knees. I close my eyes and she rubs an

122

egg lightly on each lid, its coolness burrowing through me and soothing my brain. She utters prayers, invokes the saints, and when she unfolds my hands, the eggs she has placed there glow like two oval coals.

I think the glowing eggs are no more than a feverish hallucination, but I nod appreciatively anyway when Chimuelita and la curandera leave and tell me to wait a few hours like I'll be fully recovered then. I hoped for chicken soup, not magic. I would have listened to a good story, but I'm not falling for cheap tricks anymore.

The next morning, I wake to a fever that simmers in my shoulders, legs, and head, a heat so hot it seems to boil off my eyes' moisture. I've watched a whole day of light through the slits in my venetian blinds, the sunset's bright pink, the night's yellow streetlights, the morning's white. I slept through a whole day of noise—the alarm, my neighbor's lawn mower, the squeaky school bus, the ice cream truck, the phone. It's almost night again, one full day after Chimuelita's visit, and I still can't sit up without dizziness.

I don't know what to do. I feel so helpless. Even though she fired me, I dial Susie's number, and she comes right over. For a moment, I think I'm forgiven, but when I hear her patronizing voice, I realize that it's going to take a lot more than a fever to get her sympathy.

"What happened to you?" she says. "You've got hair like a Chia pet's." She puts her hand on my forehead. "You're burning up, Sofía. What have you done for yourself?"

"I called Chimuelita."

"Chimuelita? And what did she do?"

"She used eggs," I say with a weak laugh.

Susie gets a brush and a rubber band from my room and starts combing my hair with firm, determined strokes, pulling it back in a tight ponytail that makes my temples throb. "I don't believe you," she says, half scolding. "What were you going to do? Lie here till you died?"

"I called you, didn't I?"

"You can barely talk. You don't even have over-the-counter medicine. Sometimes you're such a child."

She drives me in her new Ford Explorer, too big for her, too complicated with all its latest amenities—a CD player, air conditioning, reading lights, an alarm, a remote control that unlocks the doors from a distance. When Susie turns the key, there's no sound at all, no gear grinding or fume burping, just a polite beeping and an illuminated sign: Please Fasten Your Seatbelts. I thought her business was failing. I thought she was barely breaking even.

I don't have insurance, so she takes me to a minor emergency clinic that costs thirty dollars a visit. In the waiting room, she flips through a *Glamour* magazine while I fill out an application similar to the form I filled out at the bank. On the magazine cover is a blond woman in a tight leather bodysuit, the front zipper bursting over cleavage, a whip in her hands, the caption below saying *The Hot Days of Summer*. Susie reads "Food for Sex," studies an ad for a Caribbean cruise, and takes a quiz to determine which Maybelline makeup palette best reflects her personality.

"You want to come with me?" I say when they call my name.

"I've got to hold your hand?" she scolds, following me anyway. When she's angry, she's curt for months. Once I accidentally vacuumed up her gold bracelet. She made me open up that vacuum bag and pick through the debris and dust till I found the few mangled strands that remained. Never mind that I was cleaning her room and that she was the one who had carelessly left her bracelet on the floor. "Remember that bracelet you sucked up with the vacuum?" she'd say, and I'd hear some story about her mother saving money for it or Susie wanting to use it as an heirloom someday. I finally bought her a new one. I'll probably spend the next ten years apologizing for missing her wedding dance and yelling at her customer. Susie's forgiveness isn't easy to earn.

The butcher paper crackles when I sit on the examination bed. I smell ammonia, rubbing alcohol, and a stale diaper in the trash. A white counter lines the wall with glass containers holding gauze, cottonballs, Q-tips, wooden tongue depressors, matchbox cars, lemon drops, condoms. A chart on the wall explains the Heimlich maneuver and CPR. Another shows canker sores.

"Frank?" Susie says, clearly surprised when he walks in. "What are you doing here?"

"I work here," he says.

"You work downtown. During the day."

"I work here too, Susie. You know that."

"But you quit last month so you could go to school at night and take that review class for the MCAT exam."

"I never signed up for that class. I kept my extra job instead."

He tries turning his attention to me, but Susie won't let him.

"What happened to your dream?" she says.

"I'm trying to help you with your store."

"I don't need any help."

Frank runs a hand through his hair and shakes his head. "I can't believe you won't accept my job here," he says with a weak smile that reveals a silver tooth quickly losing its luster. "I've never lied to you. I never said I was going to be a doctor. And I'm working this second job for you. Where do you think the money's coming from? For your store? For your car? For the clothes you like to wear? Because no one's buying your stuff yet."

"What's that supposed to mean?" she says, getting in his face.

"You haven't made any money, Susie."

He's just calmly stating a fact but this last comment gets Susie all worked up. She starts arguing with him. I don't know what she says exactly because she's talking fast and incoherently, her gestures slicing the air. Poor Frank bears it patiently, though she utters enough venom to down a beast.

"I thought we talked this through, Frank."

"You told me what you want. Don't you have what you want?"

"But what about your dream?"

"I like nursing."

"But you're like a servant here," she says. "You should be the one giving the orders."

"That's enough," he says, glancing at me and feeling embarrassed.

"What kind of man are you?" she says, her voice almost yelling. "Don't you have any ambitions?"

"That's enough!" he says again, firmly.

A cold and unrelenting stare stands between them till another nurse peeks in and asks if everything's all right.

"I'm just talking to my wife," Frank says, his voice shaking. Susie shoulders aside the other nurse as she storms out the door.

"She'll get over it," he says, and I realize that this fight's not the first, that there's an ugly side to Susie and Frank, that she's got him working two jobs and enduring hell for it. What happened to her mushy puppy love act? What's she mad about, anyway? She's got to wake up and accept that her store isn't working and that Frank's not planning to study medicine. There's nothing wrong with a flea-market booth or a husband who likes nursing. Susie and Frank can make a decent living and afford to buy a house when their land-lord threatens to sell.

Frank inhales deeply to regain himself. Then he flips to my name on the clipboard, takes my temperature and blood pressure, and asks a few routine questions, his tone indifferent like I'm not Sofía anymore. The doctor comes in wearing a gray tie with red swirls that seem to gyrate like the eyes of hypnotized cartoons, but he's indifferent too. He holds a depressor over my tongue, peers into my throat, nods, and mumbles as if he can see all the hamburgers, all the fruit and ice cream, all the cookies I've eaten—as if he can see my words lurking behind the fists in my throat, the secrets I've swallowed and those I've spit out. He says I have strep throat, and then he scribbles some eight-syllable prescription.

"Take these for ten days even if you start to feel better," he says before walking out. I wish all answers were so easy—a little look-see, a few scribbled lines, a problem solved in fewer than ten days.

When I get to the front lobby, Susie's gone. Frank apologizes, tells the clerk he's taking his break, and drives me home, stopping by the pharmacy so I can pick up my prescription.

"How do these work?" I ask, looking through the vial's amber plastic at tablets that seem to glow in the dark.

Frank says, "They've got some kind of chemical that breaks up the walls of the germ cells."

"So the insides spill out?" I ask. "That's all it is?"

"Just a chemical and nothing more."

Last week I might have been disappointed, but after everything that's happened, I'm not surprised that the cure is something as ordinary as a chemical reaction. "That's what I thought," I mumble to Frank, but he's too worried about Susie to mind me.

126

As soon as I get home, I take my medicine, return to bed, and later that night, I open my eyes to the television's light flickering through my bedroom's open door. I don't remember turning the TV on. I'm hoping Julián didn't crawl in through the window again. I go toward the living room, the hall lengthening itself to an impossible stretch, as if I'm walking on the revolving floor of a treadmill machine. It seems like years before I get to the other side of my small house. My whole body aches like I've been punched unrelentingly, but the tightness in my throat is beginning to subside. When I get to the front room, I sit at my card table and imagine that David's sleeping on the couch, his feet hanging over the armrest, one arm above his head, the other twitching occasionally, a *TV Guide* on his chest and his face as still as a statue's. I'm surprised to remember him in such remarkable detail.

Looking into the scrap of wood before me, I see an apostle, sandy and sunburned from walking through the desert. He's in an oasis searching for food with a flashlight even though there's fruit on every tree and a strong sun. He thinks it's a mirage, that he's still on a sandy dune. When I feel better, I'll draw this image and call it "Doubting Thomas."

Maybe it's the medication that makes my imagination seem so solid. I try looking through David, who appears thick and electric. I imagine nerve cells firing off pictures in his brain and the treelike capillaries of his lungs, but I can't see through him. "You're so beautiful," I say, and I imagine he opens his eyes, smiles, shifts on the couch and falls asleep again. When I wake up in the morning, I feel better, and I would like to think it was looking into the wood or remembering David that cured me, but I know it was a pill breaking up cell walls.

12

Barely Four Hundred Dollars

I spent a few more days coughing and sleeping alternately on the bed and sofa, but now, a week after the prescribed ten days of antibiotics, I feel fully recovered. I haven't seen Susie since the doctor visit, and she hasn't called to ask how I'm feeling. I believe she's still mad about the wedding and embarrassed by the scene with Frank, so I'm surprised when she rings the doorbell.

When I unlatch the screen, she seems frantic, her hair a tangled mess, her blouse wrinkled and untucked, her fingernails jaggedly bitten, and her eyes raccoonlike with smudged mascara.

"What's going on?" I ask.

She answers half blubbering, "They're going to take away my store. Can you believe that?"

"Why?"

"Because that no good husband of mine used my merchandise as collateral on the startup loan and on my car."

She slumps on the couch, hides her face in her hands, falls into shoulder-shaking sobs, and all I can do is offer a tissue and stand dumbfounded. How am I supposed to help her? I don't know the first thing about running a business. I know it's selfish, but I don't like people coming to me in crisis, especially Susie, who's supposed to keep her head together.

"What do you want me to do?" I ask.

"Lend me some money, Sofía. Do I have to spell it out?"

The only money I have, besides a hundred dollars in the bank, is what I've put in my coffee can. I tell Susie she can have it.

"It's in my bedroom," I say.

"You're a godsend, Sofía." Then she runs off like a child after candy.

I know I was saving that money for the house, but what's the point? There's no way I've saved fifty thousand dollars. Mr. Vela's already finished the repairs, painted the house a clean, blinding white, and promised to replace the driveway before the week ends. I'm going to lose this place unless I get some last-minute miracle. I've known this ever since my loan was denied. I just didn't want to accept it. I wanted to pretend this place was mine until I was forced to box my things, but each day I sense the deepening inanimacy of this house. It doesn't speak anymore—doesn't creak, rustle, or drip—and its doors, cabinets, and windowsills are too perfectly straight. Sometimes I look at the welcome mat Mr. Vela's placed by the door, the little rows of flowers he's planted, the way he's straightened my haphazard lawn chairs, and I feel like I'm living on a movie set. I didn't realize that I loved my home's imperfections best, that I found its idiosyncrasies endearing.

I hear a rattling muffler, and when I look out the door, I see Julián getting out of an old car, a faded red Cutlass Supreme with a peeling white vinyl top. He scoots over to the passenger side to get out.

"The other door is stuck," he explains.

He's as ruffled as Susie, his sleeves torn, his jeans muddied, and a bruise yellowing along his brow.

"What happened to you?" I ask.

"I got in a fight," he says with his out-of-tune voice.

I let him in, and when I hand him a paper towel, I notice that his hands seem ten years older because they're callused, blistered, and full of chicken-scratch scars.

"What happened to your hands?" I ask.

"I got a job now. With this landscape man. I help him cut yards after school and on weekends."

"I thought you weren't going to get a job."

"I need the extra money, remember? I got a new car and a lot of other things."

I should be glad he's earning money now, but I'm feeling disappointed because I liked the way he'd come by to do odd jobs. He hardly does that anymore. "You should have asked if you needed more money," I say.

He leans against the doorframe, picks at the dirt beneath his nails, looks up and says, "You'd buy me a new car?"

"That thing's not new."

"It's new to me."

He's acting like a big shot now. He's taking his petty job too seriously. "So what were you fighting about?" I ask.

"We caught some guys messing with our wall, putting their tag names over our painting."

"What painting?" I say because the only thing Julián and his friends draw now are spades, little black inverted hearts on stems, scribbled on telephone poles, bus benches, curbs, convenience stores, and all over the white concrete bricks of Cole Park's amphitheater. Julián and his friends haven't drawn since I burned their backs. Like dogs pissing on trees, they just mark territory, spray-painting their boundaries with a sign as meaningless as the Watch For Ice warnings on Corpus Christi's never-frozen bridges. Their spades are hardly discernible on the sign-cluttered roads.

I'm about to ask where he fought when Susie stomps toward me with a wad of bills in one hand and my coffee can clanking with change in the other. "You barely have four hundred dollars!" she yells.

"You counted it?"

"Twice!"

"I can't believe you sat there and counted it," I say more to myself than to her.

"Where did it go?" she accuses. "Did you spend it all on him?" She points at Julián. "What did you do? Buy him candy and soda pop?"

"Hey," he says, approaching her. "I'm not some fucking little kid! I've got my own car now." He stares like he wants to punch her face.

"Leave us alone a minute," I say, urging him out. He doesn't move. He stands between Susie and me as if I needed protection. "I'll be all right," I insist, and he finally saunters off, looking back like a wary guard dog before disappearing to the restroom.

Susie puts my coffee can on the table and riffles the bills as if she could change their value the way Señor Surprise changes the faces of cards. I never needed more than it could hold before. I reached into it when I wanted to buy woodburning supplies, snacks, movie tickets, or fancy stationery from the Hallmark store. It's not like I actually fooled myself into thinking the can could hold enough money for a house. Truth is, I never knew how much could fit. I pay bills with my bank account, but this was my play money, money for wishes, not needs. I thought my Maxwell House can had power because its coffee, like a potent elixir, could take my grouchy, baggy-eyed mother and make her civil in the morning, make her hum as I got ready for school, make her say "have a good day" with mushy sincerity. Now when I look at it, its paint so rubbed down I can't even read its white letters, I have to acknowledge its limitations, that when it's filled to capacity, all it holds is barely four hundred dollars.

"Take it," I tell Susie. "I'm not going to have enough for the house, anyway."

"Well, it isn't enough to get me out of trouble, either," she says, ungratefully. "I need at least two thousand dollars."

I realize there's no difference between two thousand and fifty thousand dollars if you don't have enough, but what Susie doesn't realize is that I'm ditching my dream for her. I feel like an absolute failure right now. Susie's world is falling apart, my world's falling apart, Julián's growing up in spite of me, and I've got nothing to say.

"You were my last hope," she tells me with a look that expects an answer.

I try to salvage things. "Remember that statue in San Antonio?" I say, thinking I can be like Chimuelita by offering a good story to brush away the fear.

"The statue they said was crying?"

"It was crying," I insist. "You can ask Chimuelita. We saw it."

"Don't you ever read the paper, Sofía?"

"Sometimes," I say even though I know that glancing at the comics, the Target ads, and the TV listings isn't the same as reading the news.

"Because they figured out what was really going on," Susie says. "It was a miracle. There were priests and nuns there."

"It was a goddamn freak of nature!" she yells, exasperated. "They called in forensic scientists to test if the moisture was water or tears, and guess what, it was water. Good old H-2-O."

"So she cried water," I say. "That doesn't change anything."

"It was condensation, Sofía! Just like you get on your windows. Water had seeped into the wood, and when they turned up the heat too high, it leaked out like tears."

I don't want to believe her explanation, but it sounds too logical to be anything but true. So she's going to take that away too? First my loaves-and-fishes superstition and now my only encounter with the divine?

"You're a sad-ass friend, Susie."

"Me?" she says, standing up, clenching the dollars in one hand and pointing accusingly at me with the other while she walks toward the door. "I'm the one that's been there for you all your life, Sofía, and all you can offer is a few measly dollars and a fake sign from God?"

"Well that's all I have," I say, but she's too mad to hear me.

I just want to lie in bed and stare at the walls, but Julián's still here, sitting on the edge of the tub with a damp towel.

"I guess you got in a fight too," he says. "I was ready to twist off her snotty little nose the way she talked to you."

I take the towel from him, and when I wipe his face, the cut on his lip bleeds again so I press the cloth firmly against it, his breath warm on my knuckles. I stand there for a long time considering how rotten I've been as a friend, replaying the scene with Susie and with David too, trying to figure out how to fix things. Lost in my thoughts, I absently run my fingers through Julián's hair, oblivious when he leans into my stomach, clutches my loose blouse, bites at my buttons till I feel his sudden hot tongue on my navel. He edges up to my breasts, sets his mouth there, kneads, pinches, and fiercely sucks at them like they've got something to fill him.

When I realize that I'm feeling dispassionate, that Julián's nothing more than a pesky fly because I'm too worried about Mr. Vela selling the house, Susie emptying my can, David never visiting the restaurant anymore, and Pete acting like an iron-fisted boss ever since César left, I understand what my mother felt when all those men groaned and sweated in her bed. She wasn't angry, bitter, or even sad. I think she became acutely aware of how much empty space and how many empty words lie between people. Her sex was a desperate act, a way of insisting that someone notice her, and when it didn't work, when she realized her lovers were intent upon their own bodies, their own pleasures, she surrendered to the world's indifference.

I can't preserve that pristine image of Julián anymore, keep him dustless like a butterfly in a glass dome. He's got a job now, drives a car, and tags walls. His hands edge the rim of my pants and he says, "I want to finger-fuck you." When I look at him, the persistent way he fumbles with my jeans, the thickening Adam's apple, and the pale beginnings of a moustache, his insatiable leanness represents to me not infinite, but a collapsed potential. The walls of my tiny bathroom seem suddenly cavernous and the floor seems a well's depth below, and all that lies between us is his desire—and space.

"You better go," I say, backing away and closing my shirt.

"Why?" he asks, that childish tenacity returning. "You're breaking up with me?"

"Sure," I say, though it sounds ridiculous now. "I'm breaking up."

"You're telling me I can't come over anymore?"

"I have to move out, anyway," I say.

I'm thinking things are calm and amicable, that we're being real adults, but when he gets to my living room, he plants himself on the sofa and starts pleading. He uses every manipulative technique his teenage mind can muster from the self-pitying I'm-not-good-enough-for-you to the desperate I'll-kill-myself. The more he begs for an answer or an acceptance, the more disgusted with myself I become. I befriended him because I thought he was honest, and he probably is in spite of his gangbanger friends. I'm the one who fed his infatuation. What was I thinking? I'm supposed to act like an adult.

"Look, you better go before it gets any worse," I say.

He still searches for answers. "Is it my car?" he asks. "You don't like my car?"

"No, that isn't it."

"My friends then? You want me to ditch them?"

"No."

"Then what is it? What did I do?"

"You didn't do anything, Julián. We're just wrong. Look at yourself. Look at me. I don't even know if you're seventeen yet."

"It's about age then?"

"Yes, that's a big part of it."

"So what was all that stuff at the beach? Why were you always letting me over? You've been playing me or what?"

"Yes, Julián. I've been playing you. I'm a stupid, foolish woman playing around with a kid."

This "kid" comment hits a nerve. There's nothing Julián resents more than being patronized. He stands up and paces for one angry minute. Then he throws me the most hateful look, kicks the table, and knocks over my can. I watch its change trickle out.

"You bitch!" he yells, slamming the door and peeling out the driveway in his new beat-up car.

And I don't feel anything—no sickness, no anger, no desire, no love. I want to sleep, not to dream, but to forget, to fake death for a while because I'm tired of wrestling with myself. Maybe Susie's right. Maybe I should diversify.

I heat my pyroelectric pen, take scraps of wood and draw Mickey Mouse, Tweety Bird, and write García, Flores, Smith. They're easy to draw because there's no detail or shading. Maybe I can open my own flea market booth, take the initiative for once, make some money. I don't think it would kill me to draw against the lines, but then I see the curve of Mickey Mouse's ear lacerating a saint's arm and the calligraphy like a chain-link fence crosshatching the images beneath.

13

Bishop Zumárraga

The next day, there's a Closed sign on Pete's door, and when I walk in, he's sharing a beer with César as if his absence hasn't been a wide chasm we had walked around. A quiet laughter flows easily between them, and I notice that Pete's clenched brows have finally relaxed.

"What's going on?" I ask.

"We're going to have a party," Pete says, playfully punching his son's shoulder. "Go call Parker," he adds, and César runs up the stairs. I don't know what to think. Pete's anger seemed like a sea he'd never cross. I study his intent, gray-flecked brows and his neck's mole, dark and plump like a gorging tick.

"I guess you were right," I say. "César came back."

"No, no," he answers, reaching in his pocket. "I had to call him first."

He hands me a graduation announcement, an unsentimental card with the year puckered on the front and with a sketch of Del Mar topping the commencement's details written in compact black letters. Only the date and César's name stand out. There isn't even a personal note in it, but somehow Pete imagines a deeper implication, reads between its lines, and finds a hope to cling to.

"I don't get it," I say. "How does this fix things? César's still with Parker. Isn't that the reason you threw him out?"

"That's what I thought," Pete says, tugging his sideburns, "but César never liked school. We fought a thousand times because I couldn't see why he would want to waste his brains on a shrimp boat when he had a chance for something better."

"But he went to school anyway," I say.

"I know. That's the thing. Ever since I got this card I wondered why he kept going especially after that night, especially because it wasn't what he wanted." He reads the card again, his face pensive. "I thought he was against me. I thought this thing with Parker was a way to spite me, but it isn't about me at all. He went to school because I'm his father. You understand?"

"No," I say.

"He accepted my ways, Sofía, and if I want him in my life, I have to accept his. Things aren't perfect like they show in the movies. You have to meet people halfway. Like you."

"Me?"

He tousles my hair like I'm some nine-year-old with a good report card. "I know you'd rather be lazy around here, but you really picked up the slack when we needed you."

"Because you threatened me," I say. I might have worked hard after Pete and Chimuelita yelled at me, but I did it grudgingly, whining under my breath and throwing mean looks at Pete's back. He heard me once, mocking his stern orders, but when I caught his eye and the offended expression there, he turned away without mentioning it. He makes it sound like he's lucky to have me, like I chose to work hard. I don't deserve his praise. He's just seeing what he wants to see.

He squints against the setting sun. "Close the front blinds, will you?" he says, but before I reach them, Chimuelita storms in, cradling two fish wrapped in butcher paper, their heads and tails peeking, their eyes flat and silver like dimes. She looks at us and lets out an exasperated sigh.

"Three hours gone," she complains. "I went like you told me, cabrón, all the way to Port Aransas to see Mr. Martínez about these fish."

"Well, it looks like you found him," Pete laughs.

"Let me tell you something," she says to me. "That Mr. Martínez has a thing for me. He gave me flirty looks and said I looked delicious in this dress. What kind of talk is that for a married woman?"

"I'm sure you can take care of yourself," I laugh.

"You're damn right. I had to slap him with this tail." She waves it at us.

"You slapped him?" Pete says. "That's no way to bargain. Did he give you a good price anyway?"

"A good price? That's why you sent me over?"

"He's been eyeing you for over thirty years."

"¡Cabrón!" she yells, rushing toward him, the fish slipping from her arms and sliding on the floor toward Pete's shoes.

"Calm down," he says. "I've got something serious to tell you."

She gives him a suspicious look. "No me eches mentiras," she warns.

But Pete's face beams. "César's come home," he says, laughing and pursuing when Chimuelita runs happy circles around the bar, the floor creaking with their weight. She disappears behind the kitchen door and Pete follows, waving a big wooden spoon. They're clumsy, their bodies making things fall from the shelves, their laughter mingled with the racket of pots and pans. When I finally catch up to them, Pete's kissing her toothless mouth, patting her nalgas, and saying "mi Chimuelita" over and over again.

"Looks like things worked out," I say, but they're too love-drunk to hear.

After closing the front blinds, picking up a few things in the restaurant, and watching Chimuelita smother César with affection, we go upstairs where I make a cornmeal batter for the fish while Chimuelita lops off their heads and tails, peels away their scales, and frees pinkish meat from their bones. Before we can heat the grease, the family arrives. The upstairs kitchen is a tight closet compared to the one below, so I get jabbed by elbows tossing salads, stirring casseroles, or buttering Tía Lupe's homemade bread. Children run between our legs, cling to my jeans, give pleasured squeals when I put tidbits in their mouths. Every burner is on. One of the daughters stands before the open fridge to cool off. She refills our glasses with chilled dark wine as we cook.

In the dining room, the men extend the table and carry up chairs from the restaurant. Pete opens the hutch to remove some china. "Sofía," he says, "when I went to that fancy store to buy these dishes, those people looked at me like I was a flea-bitten dog. I had more than eight hundred dollars. I wasn't going to get married without buying a whole set for my wife—not just dinner plates but the gravy boat and soup tureen and salt and pepper shakers. Look at this." He lifts a tiny cup that looks too delicate for his bear-claw hand. "This here is a demitasse, a fancy word for coffee cup."

"Tell her what happened," César says.

"I pointed at everything I wanted, and the salesman asked if I had enough credit at their store. You should have seen his eyes when I paid cash. I showed him up. I didn't need his lousy credit."

"And they were careless with your dishes, weren't they, Dad?"

"I swear I heard china crumbling as I drove off. Maybe I wasn't a successful businessman yet. Maybe I was still rough around the edges. But I worked hard for those dishes."

"These ones?" I say. "Because they look okay to me."

"That's what I'm saying—no breaks, no cracks—and they weren't even packed right."

"It was meant to be," Chimuelita says, and everyone nods in agreement. "Our prayers were answered. Like with César here."

I enjoy cooking and listening to stories, but when Chimuelita mentions prayer, a bitter indignation wells up in me. I've spent the last several months begging for a home and nothing's happened. I've wasted dollars on the lottery without even matching one number.

I say, "César's here because Pete called him over."

"God made him call," Chimuelita corrects.

"No, He didn't," I say.

She cups my face with her hands and whispers, "How can you say that? You—who fainted before the statue?"

"The statue that was crying?" I move her hands and laugh wryly when I remember what Susie said about the scientists.

"Remember that La Virgen promised to fix things with César and Pete," she says, full of conviction.

"She did? And what did she say, exactly?"

Chimuelita gives me a hard, angry look. "What's the matter with you, Sofía? You think I'm making this up? There are reasons for things. Reasons for fainting in churches."

"Yes," I say. "I had the shakes from being hungry and the church was stuffy too. Falling before that statue was a damn coincidence, Chimuelita." Why can't she see that? Sometimes things are simply strokes of good or bad luck, and miracles are more imagination than fact.

"There are all kinds of knowing," she says. "Not just words, but visions too. You think I would lie about a thing like that?" She turns her back to me. She won't discuss this anymore.

I'm convinced that nothing really happened at that church. When I fainted, there was green, then black, then smelling salts beneath my nose. I'm ready to debate this further when I notice how motionless, how silent the family suddenly becomes. Even the children seem suspended. I realize that I've broken some rule by making Chimuelita turn her back. I come to understand that in this house, without question, Pete and Chimuelita have the ultimate word.

The movement and noise doesn't resume until Pete sets the table. He places the china gently and meticulously arranges the plates, bowls, and silverware. He centers an ornate candelabra and lights its candles while everyone stands back to watch. I'm tickled by his small adjustments—the way he wipes his smudges from the glassware and folds the linen.

When Parker arrives, we're too afraid to break the sudden silence, but he seems composed, undaunted. He makes us wait for an unbearable minute before smiling and asking, "What do you call a circle of blondes, Pete?"

"I don't know," Pete answers.

"A dope ring."

"A dope ring?" Pete repeats, perplexed. He contemplates the answer, and when he finally gets the joke, he laughs hard, holding his belly to keep it from jiggling. He puts a hand on Parker's shoulder while he fails at his own blonde joke. "It's better in Spanish," he laughs.

Then he fetches Parker a beer and spills the stories and the wrestling news he's kept bottled up, their laughter as forthcoming and boisterous as before, their months of anger forgotten. I wish Susie's forgiveness were as easy. When I tried calling, a nervous Frank said she was sleeping, but I know better. Susie plans to make me beg. I have to decide if our friendship is worth it.

Frustrated by the crowded kitchen, Chimuelita throws us out, and I find a quiet corner where I watch the family settling into its rhythm. Tía Lupe is already teaching a young nephew basic guitar chords. The children make toys of rugs, frames, and paper sacks. Occasionally, they play too roughly, and their mothers are quick to kiss their mild injuries. Pete's sons stand awkwardly against the walls, their boots almost causing a dozen accidents. They seem charmed by their wives. This moment would be perfect if David were here.

It's finally time to eat, and the two fish are enough to feed the whole family. We pass the food around and serve ourselves copious spoonfuls. Then at the moment Chimuelita bites into her bread, we hear a snap followed by a trickle of blood and a molar.

"Aha!" she says, cleaning the tooth on her blouse, holding it to the candlelight, and letting it flicker for a few moments before waving it in my face. "Tell me this is a coincidence!" she says. "Tell me this isn't a sign!"

What sign? I feel like saying because the only signs I believe are those that advertise like Selena on Pete's wall or the spade on Julián's back. Chimuelita thinks we live in an intricate web where one distant corner tugs another, where unrelated events exert their gravities in a mystical chain reaction. Random facts present themselves—moisture appears on a statue's cheek, César comes home, and Chimuelita bites into a hard loaf. I can't see beyond what's provable—condensation, forgiveness, and a cavity finally giving way.

Pete brings in the mayonnaise jar, opens the cap, and when Chimuelita drops the tooth, it settles on a nest of her other fallen "signs."

14

Good to the Last Drop

The next day, I hear Mr. Vela's rhythmic scouring as he smoothes the cement he's poured over my driveway shells. It's hot. There aren't any clouds and the sun's relentless glare pains the eyes, but I don't offer anything. I saw the mallet in his truck and the For Sale sign. He can get his own water if he wants. It's his house, isn't it? I mind my own business till I hear the trowel drop and Mr. Vela calling for me in an out-of-breath voice. When I peek outside, he's leaning against the house and clutching his shirt where his heart is. I can't stay angry when I see how vulnerable he is.

"You OK?" I say, running up to him.

"I think it's too hot for me."

"You want me to call your wife?"

"No. She gets too worried. She'll take me to the hospital when all I have is heartburn."

He puts his hand on my shoulder, and even though he leans on me, I hardly notice his weight. He's got creaky bones, tissue-thin skin, and dark roly-poly veins on his forearms. He's shorter than I remember and thinner too. He breathes in deeply before climbing the porch stairs and supporting his weight on an armrest when he lowers his tired body to the couch.

"What do you want me to do?" I ask, feeling helpless.

"Can you get me a glass of water and some aspirin?"

I hurry back with a tall glass, two aspirins, and a damp towel. He takes a long time finishing the water, but when he's done, he seems a little revived. He even removes his cowboy hat to fan his face.

"I'm too old to be working so hard," he says.

"You should have hired some men like you did with the painting."

"I thought about it, but it's a lot of money for something I can do myself." He asks me to sit down by patting the cushion beside him. "I wouldn't sell this place," he explains, "if I could still afford the taxes, if I could still fix things when they break down, but I'm retired already—and tired. I've always wanted to take that trip without worrying about the time. You understand?"

"Yes," I say because there are things I'd like to do without worrying about time—like drawing.

"When I was trying to rent this house, I was asking for more than your mother could afford. But there she was with a little girl and nowhere to go. I never made a cent off this place, but your mother was like a daughter and you like a grandchild. It really hurts that you won't visit anymore."

As he talks, I begin to understand that Mr. Vela has wanted to sell this house for a long time, that he was waiting for me to . . . to . . . to grow up. I've been foolish believing that his decision to sell was a decision against me and that my bitching wasn't meant to hurt him the way a taunting teenager hurts her parents. I don't want to be like Susie, who wants her dreams on her own terms, who's willing to disown a loving husband and a best friend when things don't go her way. I love Mr. Vela. I think about Pete, how unwittingly wise he is. "It isn't about me," he said, and he was trying to say that the world is vaster than us.

After my mother died, my hands were cupped, not for water or communion, but for the vomit I felt rising in my throat. I didn't know I'd have to shop so much, that the funeral director would put me in a skinny elevator cage and drop me into a basement with piped-in organ music where he kept his polished coffins like used cars on a sale lot. He made a sweeping gesture over his showcase of coffins, no different than the salesmen on late-night commercials. It was nothing but another store. I got sick when I discovered that each of the funeral plans had a price too. The thought of buying a ceremony made me throw up all over the leather wing chair. "It's OK," the funeral director said, "we see this all the time."

I was only eighteen, fatherless, without grandparents, as far as I knew. Who could I call but Mr. Vela? He came right over, even wore a suit, and very professionally negotiated the cost of things. When they put my mother in the ground, I heard strangers weeping like she had been the whole point of their lives, but Mr. Vela wept in a truer way—I'm sure I saw it, a streak of moisture trickling down his cheek.

He puts his arm around me because he sees the tears I'm trying to blink away. "It's nothing," he says, shushing me as I clench my lips against years of trapped grief. How could I have been so stubborn? How could I have risked losing the man who fixed my ballerina, who gave me a Suburban he could have earned some money for, who cried when my mother died? I don't know what a family is, but maybe it's this moment of utter forgiveness—like the easy way Parker and César laughed with Pete. I sink into Mr. Vela's frail shoulder, my crying a pure sound that exists for itself and only for itself like a door's creak or the gulp of a bathtub's drain.

So now I have a cement driveway like everyone else on this street—smooth, flat, slick cement that's perfect for hopscotch, roller skates, Matchbox cars, chalk-drawn buildings and parking lots. Maybe a family will move in and play those games here. After Mr. Vela leaves, I search for that one soft spot where I can sink my palms. With a stick I write my name. It will harden and remain permanently, unlike the lines I burned on the house's walls. I can return five or ten years from now and still see SOFÍA LOREN SAUCEDA.

A car startles me, and when I look up, I see David parking his Honda at the curb. "What are you doing?" he asks, coming to stand beside me. We haven't spoken in months and his voice seems brand new.

"Writing my name," I say.

The late sun makes our shadows lie long and his melts into mine even though we are standing apart. He picks up a rock, skips it across the street. Large silences lie interspersed between our words.

"You feeling better?" he asks.

"You knew I was sick?"

"Sure. I spent the whole night here. Remember?"

"You did?" I say because I thought I was dreaming. "You weren't here in the morning."

"I had to go to work. I didn't mean to stay, but you weren't thinking straight. You had your front door flapping open while you slept. Anybody could've walked in."

"So Frank called you? He told you I was feeling bad?"

"No, I came because you were stalking me at work."

"I wasn't stalking you," I say.

"Sure you were." He's tickled. Mentioning the day I parked across his school makes him squint. Makes me squint too. I thought I was hallucinating the night I saw him sleeping on my couch, but here he is, standing before me, telling me that he was really here.

"The house is for sale now?" he asks nodding toward the sign Mr. Vela and I posted in the grass.

"Yes."

"Where are you going to live?"

"I don't know yet. I'll find a place. An apartment, maybe."

"You okay with that?"

"Yes," I say realizing that the ceiling fan's pull chain, the bedpost's rosary, my father's photographed shadow, and the lingering echoes of my mother's complaints are a thick vein of her insistence that every hope is a false illusion, and every unasked-for act of charity a sinister you-owe-me. I don't want to be like my mother. I realize that Mr. Vela expects no payback for my years of living cheap and that David's standing before me like a materialized dream.

"You hungry?" he asks as we walk inside.

"Yes."

I go to my room, sit on the bed's edge, kick off my sandals, intending to change shoes, but when he kneels at my bare feet and presses his thumb firmly along the arch of my foot, a slow quiver meanders its way through me.

146

"We could eat later," I say, leaning to kiss him. This time there's no hesitancy and I accept his body's full weight and the way our clothes gently cascade off our hips and shoulders and that raw, sunburned feel when he enters me with a quiet urgency and a depth that leaves no space between us. He's gentle and cautious at first, but we reach a rhythm that leaves us light-headed, that sweeps away all fear till I know only this one certainty—that the only home I need is this tight circle of arms.

In the late afternoon, the sunlight lies horizontally across the room. I see a few wispy strands on David's knuckles, relish the newborn feel of them against his callused hands. I peer at the lines on his fingers and palms.

"David," I say, excited.

"What?"

"I see saints in your hands."

He holds them up and tries to see the saints too, but I can tell from his skeptical expression that he can't see beyond his finger-prints, that seeing saints in random swirls is as unfathomable to David as Chimuelita's falling teeth are to me. Is it possible? Am I some kind of Percival Lowell insisting on an order where none exists? Forging causality like Chimuelita, who pays a tooth for every imaginary miracle? Maybe the people who draw against lines do so unintentionally because they don't recognize what's there. But I see them everywhere—saints in tree trunks, in walls, in the ripples of the bed's crumpled sheets, in the woodlike rings of David's fingerprints.

He eventually gives up.

He changes the subject. "Is this your coffee can?" he asks, lift-ing it from the dresser.

"Yes."

He shakes it playfully like a child with maracas, tells me to close my eyes. "Hear that? Hear that?"

"You're being silly," I laugh.

"What? I can't hear you!"

He shakes the can harder, louder, the bell-like clanging of nick-els and dimes floating about me like flakes of silver manna falling from God's sky.

147

Diana López was born and raised in Corpus Christi, Texas. She is a graduate of the creative writing program at Southwest Texas State University, San Marcos. She currently lives in San Antonio where she has worked as both a medical lab technician and, more recently, an eighth-grade English teacher for the city's oldest school district.

Photo credit: Tricia Sebastian